I0640713

William Leighton

At the court of King Edwin

A drama

William Leighton

At the court of King Edwin
A drama

ISBN/EAN: 9783743311251

Manufactured in Europe, USA, Canada, Australia, Japa

Cover: Foto ©Andreas Hilbeck / pixelio.de

Manufactured and distributed by brebook publishing software
(www.brebook.com)

William Leighton

At the court of King Edwin

KING EDWIN.

A DRAMA.

BY

WILLIAM LEIGHTON, Jr.,

AUTHOR OF "THE SONS OF GODWIN."

PHILADELPHIA:

J. B. LIPPINCOTT & CO.

1878.

TO

MY FATHER AND MOTHER.

PREFACE.

WHEN, nearly a year ago, "The Sons of Godwin" was published, the almost simultaneous appearance of "Harold" seems to have led certain readers, who were ignorant of the dates of the issue of these books, to the supposition that the latter work suggested the former. That such was not the case the author takes this opportunity to declare. His volume had been issued two weeks when "Harold" was published, and his stereotype plates were made when a newspaper paragraph first informed him of the name and subject of Mr. Tennyson's poem.

This fact is probably of little interest to the reading public, as the celebrity and genius of the English author made his book at once an object of interest and admiration, and may have placed the contemporaneous poem on the same theme in the position of an unexpected intruder.

To those who so view his book, the author has only this apology: when he offered the work of his unprac-

7

tised pen he was ignorant that England's most honored poet designed to illustrate the same epoch and group of characters with the power and grace of his matchless verse.

Without intending an essay upon dramatic literature, the author desires to say a few words in introduction of the poem which occupies the following pages.

The announcement on the title-page is "a drama"; but the work has been written without especial reference to the requirements of the theatre, and hence will perhaps be found, in many essential respects, unsuited to stage-use. When a dramatic piece is declared unsuitable for the theatre, such unfitness has frequently been urged against it as destructive of literary value. In other words, it has been claimed that a drama means a play for the stage, and is worthy of consideration only when in theme, construction, language, and situations it is adapted for successful presentation in the theatre.

If such be the inflexible meaning of the word, drama, the author has been unfortunate in its use, and should have selected some such half-way term as dramatic poem for his title; but he has been led into error, if error it be, by the belief that the broad title, drama, covers more than the small area of the stage.

That drama means action, the derivation of the word

and its common use indicate ; yet there seems to be no good reason why this "action" should be restricted to the stage. Action, as applied to dramatic literature, signifies the presentation and unfolding of character and events, which are brought about by the meeting and intercourse of the persons of the story, and can be shown as surely, if not as effectively, on the printed page as behind the footlights of a theatre. Dramatic action may largely mean, not the actor's counterfeit presentment, but the actual movement of plot or story in the expression of thoughts, imaginations, peculiarities of character, emotion, discoveries, and all the circumstances that arise in the dialogue or soliloquy of the dramatis personæ.

The stage possesses, in its mimic illusions, wonderful fascination, by the aid of which Drama has doubtless won her most brilliant successes; but, though thus indebted to the theatre, must she, in gratitude, yield herself, the thrall of glitter and tinsel, and know no life beyond the boundaries of its painted scenes? I think not so. Wherever peculiar and striking characterizations, passions, and fancies of mankind are exhibited in the dialogue of those who are themselves the personages whose thoughts, feelings, and action make the chief interest,—there drama may be said to exist: but if dialogue refer to persons and circumstances not immediately connected with the speakers, and excite no emotion in them, such conversation can scarcely be termed dramatic, even if it take place on the most brilliantly-lighted stage; nor can the complication of such speakers produce a drama, though they relate events of great interest to audience or readers.

The dramatic form of composition seems an obvious method, suggested by nature, of illustrating its movement. Its chief advantages over narrative consist in a verisimilitude to fact, and the elimination of the author; success being largely dependent on keeping this personage, like the manipulator of Mr. Punch in the puppet-show, entirely out of sight. Whoever tells a story mingles himself and his opinions insensibly or purposely with what he relates in such manner that his presence is apparent; we see people and events consciously through his eyes and thoughts, not with our own; and therefore the story is put further away from us than when the characters appear to speak unprompted their own opinions and feelings.

This brief explanation will serve to show what the author believes to be the nature and capability of dramatic composition, and that he deems it a legitimate method of reproducing historical or imaginative scenes for general readers.

" Another play unsuited to the stage"—this is often the verdict of the critics upon the advent of a new drama ; and those who render it, with others who accept criticism in unhesitating belief, seem to imagine that a drama, stigmatized by such verdict, is thereby ostracized from literature ; while many are ready to explain the exact boundaries of stage-action, beyond which frowns a bottomless pit wherein fall all who exceed, or come short of, their prescribed limits.

Standing on the verge of this frightful abyss, into which so many gay hopes, great ambitions, and glowing fancies have fallen, listen to the faint whispers that come up, and peer into the gloom for phantoms of characterizations that flit above this, their yawning grave—Dramas unsuited to the modern stage ! Out of the shadows beneath come the agony of Prometheus, the chant of the old Greek chorus, the craze of Gretchen, the despair of Faust, the mutterings of dishonored Sampson, the poetry of gay Comus.

Suitability to the modern stage, outside of which there is for the dramatist—nothing ! This is true if he write only for the theatre ; but may not an author present his story in dramatic form for the sake of more vivid realization, and name his work, a drama, even if he has chosen such scenes as are unsuitable to the stage, and intends his book for general readers ?

AN ANTIQUE TIME.

Twelve centuries ago.—Trace back the years,
And count their spectres, as weird shapes arise
Out of old records—ah, how vast appears
The long array to our bewildered eyes!
But when we reach the dim and cloudy edge
Of history, lo! mingling with the real,
Are strange, wild figures which those old times fledge
With the miraculous plumage of th' ideal.
Back in remembrance comes the storied scene
Of ancient legend; fairy forms glide by;
The dragon rolls his pictured shape between
The sage enchanter and the giant high.
Out of such times my drama takes a day—
A posy plucked out of an ancient May.

DRAMATIS PERSONÆ.

EDWIN, King of Deira.

EDILBERGA, his queen.

ENID, Princess of Gwynedd.

PENDA, King of Mercia.

BRIAN, Prince of Gwynedd.

BLECCA, Earl of Lincoln.

PAULINUS, the queen's bishop.

COIFI, high-priest of Odin.

PELLITUS, the king's magician.

GOLDDIN, the house-thegn.

DAGBERT, a jailer.

RHYN, a Cymrian, the slave of Pellitus.

Captain of the king's guard. Deiran and Mercian lords, Christian priests, priests of Odin, ladies-in-waiting and queen's attendants, guards and king's attendants.

Date of the story, the seventh century.

Time occupied by the action, twenty-four hours.

Scene, the king's palace at York.

14

AT THE COURT OF KING EDWIN.

AT THE

COURT OF KING EDWIN.

ACT I.

SCENE I.—HALL-OF-WAITING IN THE PALACE.

PAULINUS *and* COIFI.

COIFI.

I shall see midnight looks in many faces;
And low-born carles, whose heads have bent to me,
Veiling bold eyes in superstitious fear,
Will twist gnarled, stupid brows into black frowns,
Shake heads, and mutter at th' unfaithful priest;
While thegn and ealdorman, with covert sneer,
May curl the lip, more insolent than frown.

PAULINUS.

You must find solace in sweet Enid's eyes,
Payment for sneers upon her curling lip,

And bear down vulgar gaze by the authority
Of kingly office.

COIFI.

Ay, to be a king

Is better than, a priest ; but not so safe.
These Cymrian mountaineers are hard to rule,
As rough and tameless as hill-foxes, wolves ;
They may refuse me utterly, and snarl
In harsh defiance of King Edwin's will.

PAULINUS.

Refuse you ? ay ; but not your Cymrian wife,
Who bears in delicate veins the blood of kings.
King Edwin gives them back their ruling stock
Grafted upon the Saxon.   If they snarl,
His hand will whip them to obedient smiles,
Making them bow before your vassal throne—
Vassal alone in name and in the help
That he, the great Bretwalda, lends.

COIFI.

But she,

The Cymrian princess that King Edwin gives
With Gwynedd's kingdom, loves me not ; perhaps,—
Yea, what more likely ?—she may plot against me
To fill my place with one, her countryman ;

So, while I sleep secure, Murder's red hand
Will strike, and Edwin's power bring help too late.

PAULINUS.

It is a risk that all must take who wed ;
There may be poison mingled with the honey.

COIFI.

But there is honey ; I will take the risk.

Aside.

This captive's wondrous beauty draws me on
As bears are lured by sweets until they step
On the frail twigs that hide a yawning pit,
Then fall, the hunters' prey.

To PAULINUS.

Ay, tell the king :
I will give up my gods, declare them false,
Take in their place your Christ and holy saints,
And do his will; so he fulfil your promise,
Giving me Enid and the throne of Gwynedd.

PAULINUS.

He will do so.   Although I buy your help
At price of fond desires, that, by such means,

Many may come to know the larger life
I offer; yet that life is not so bought.
It comes when Faith shall reach adoring hands
To Christ, the Saver—comes, a richer gift,
O Coifi, than delighting joys of pleasure,
Or dignity of kings.   The soul of man,
If he shall win for it eternal life
In Christ's high kingdom, is a priceless jewel,
A sparkle of Divinity's pure light,
And all things else that he most covets here,
Wealth, pleasures, power, are feasting of his sense,
Garments and viands for a holiday.
Seek not then fiercely for inferior things,
Leaving the jewel, truth, to gather up
In eager haste by armfuls worthless dirt,
Will stain you now, and weigh you down forever.

COIFI.

My mind is dull to see what you would show;
Perhaps my gods, in very jealousy,
Have filled my brain with clouds to hide your truth;
For sometimes when I ponder on the things
You tell, and after, sleep; then, in a dream,
Will Odin come, and frown; but all the while,
Knowing it is a dream, I fear him not;
For, save in dreams, he stands as still as stone.

I marvel he should come to me in dreams,
Who, to each wakeful question, answers not ;
Nor seems more sensible than the poised blocks
Set up by Cymrians in their Druid-rings.

PAULINUS.

He is a myth. 'It is the common foe
Of all mankind haunts you in Odin's shape ;
Evil can glide into each sculptured form,
And stir the inert stone or painted wood,
Scaring the world with hideous masquerade,
Affrighting men by making animate
The figures fashioned by their fear and folly.
Here is a cross ; wear it upon your breast,
And Odin will disturb your dreams no more.

COIFI.

I do not fear him ; but will wear your cross,
Lest in his rage he send down Thor, the thunderer,
To strike me with his hammer.

PAULINUS.

          Myths ! brave Coifi ;
There is no Thor, but such as fancy shapes ;
His thunder, but a legendary fable
Born of the devil to stuff the brains of men,

Leaving no place to fill with honest truth;
A noisy fable, stolen from the Greek.

COIFI.

Ay, so you say; and I must ev'n believe it;
But if there be no Thor, no gods in Asgard,
Who did the deeds recorded of our Æsir,
The sons of Bor, and the Frost-giant race?

PAULINUS.

They are delusions of the arch-enemy,
Old fables whispered down from sire to son
Until antiquity hath stamped the myths
With a traditionary blazoning
That flames like truth.

COIFI.

        I'll spend more thought upon it,
That I may come to see the Æsir race
Fly from the presence of your crucified God—

Enter PELLITUS.

The wizard Pellitus! Once more I promise
To be obedient to the king's demands.
Ho, Pellitus! what say the stars?

PELLITUS.
                                    My lords,—
Two of the arch-priests of the upper courts
Should better know each purpose of the gods
Than I can read it on this lower plain.

PAULINUS.

'Tis true—your cunning tells for once the truth:
You are indeed upon a lower plain
Too far beneath the heavenly purposes
To catch their meaning.   Break your wizard-staff;
Look on the stars as God's bright promises,
His lights that shine from mansions of the blest;
The flight of birds, His lesson to the wise,
Telling how nature moves instinct with force
And harmony, breathed from a kindly heaven,
And bearing kindliness and love to life.
Your philters, incantations, spectres, spells—
I need not tell you what to think of these;
You know your own machinery too well
To deem it truth.
                        Coifi, the gates of Truth
Are wide and bright; but many see them not;
Open your eyes, and walk not in the dark;
Think of my words; nor waste your time in talk
With this deceiver.   Farewell to you, both.
                                    Exit PAULINUS.

COIFI.

Magician, is your wand a useless staff,
To scare the ignorant?   I think it is;
Or it would flame with wrath at him who scoffs
At it and you.

PELLITUS.

Nay; this proud priest doth tell
Of the humility and love he teacheth,
Sets up his image of a god of Peace,
And in its name makes war on all the world,
Forgetful, or regardless, that his faith
Hath gathered up the scattered elements
Of mild philosophies; but shaping these
Into a presentation figure, on whose brow
Is haloed Love, would force this sad-faced god
Upon the world by intrigue and the sword.
Love and humility are only tenets,
Not active principles of this, his faith.
But wisdom long hath known a better policy
Than flaming wrath; and, though I name it not
Love or humility, can still restrain
My magic slaves, and let this railer work
A wiser purpose than his vaunted "truth."

COIFI.

You set your "wisdom" up against his "truth";

But truth and wisdom both are unseen things
The world must take on trust.

PELLITUS.
                                        Ay, for a time,
Until familiarity shall change
The trust to a belief, and call it faith.
Meantime I watch, and wait, and read the stars,
And summon phantoms from the darkest shades
Of nether Tartarus,—disembodied things
Whose reach of sight is forward, as in us
Memory goes backward on the track of years,—
Who map for me the filling up of time,
But oft with gaps and blank obscurities
That baffle certainty.   There is success,
There is defeat—both written of this faith
Paulinus flaunts with such a lofty scorn
Of all beside.   But, priest of Odin, thou
Art written down in my foretelling runes:
How thou wouldst sell, for Gwynedd's vassal throne
And Cymrian Enid, ancient Cimbric faith;
How thou wouldst bow thy purchased kingliness,
Unkingly, kneeling at Paulinus' cross—
Beware! my messengers have whispered me
Of angry Odin's vengeance; and I see,
As in a picture, a huge, prostrate cross,
And one beneath it, crushed by its dead weight.

COIFI.

A picture built of words.   Know, knave magician,
Not even Odin's self, if he could rise,
Splendid in all his panoply of arms,
And rail at me, would move me from my purpose.

PELLITUS, *aside.*

If he could rise!—this thick-skulled priest doth scoff
At superstition's might;—the world grows old.

COIFI.

For your dark hints that teem with pregnant fate;
I hear them as I listen to the thunder,
A threatening noise that roars, but harms me not.

PELLITUS.

Ay, like the thunder are my words; they harm not,
But tell of powers that hover o'er our heads,
In whose great hands the little fates of men
Are like small motes of dust a great storm whirls
Tempestuously between low skies and earth.
You fear not thunder? When the mountains shake,
Is it but empty sound that fills the air?
When the forked lightning darts among the clouds,
Or leaps to earth to shatter a great oak,
You do not fear? nor doth the threatened oak,

Because its idle limbs and foolish leaves
Have no intelligence.   Oh, we may shape
In our capricious minds forms wonderful
Of deity, and yet that deity
Is far more wonderful than wonder's shapes!
Look!   I will laugh with you at Odin's form,
But not at Odin's self, if in his shape
You picture Him that thunders.

COIFI.
That is Thor.

PELLITUS.

Odin or Thor—the names are idle nothings;
But there is That is greater than man's thought,
Vaster than he hath scope of picturing,
Though all his deities be blent in one.

COIFI.

I am not wont to tremble with weak fears.

PELLITUS.

Nor I to prate of gods.
I speak the truth; my words are harmless to you;
Nor have I enmity to poison speech
With ill; let me bring help, not any harm;
For I have that, born of my magic powers,

Potent for good or ill as it is used,
Foreknowledge.   Lo ! as on a burnished shield
I see the pictures of the future pass ;
I see you go, a fond, deluded fool,
Into a pit that yawns before your feet ;
Nor yet so blind as not to see the snare,
And yet so blind to fall into the snare.

COIFI.

I will not hear it ; you have learned this thing
By common knowledge, and would fright me off
From what I would, for reasons that I know not.
One thing, magician, let me tell you here,
Lest they, your messengers, forget to tell it :
'Tis waste of words to picture threats to Coifi ;
He may be blind, a fool, but not a coward.
There is my purse ; if you have meant me well,
My thanks ; if ill, I care not.   So, farewell.

Exit COIFI.

PELLITUS.

Even this stupid priest of Odin scorns me ;
My footing stands upon a slippery ground
Unless I may control such minds as his,
Or if the beast-like courage of his heart
Can prove a talisman to mock my skill.
No, it is this : he hath been offered bribes

So great, their very greatness hides all else.
The Christian bishop hath a subtle mind,
Nor scorns the help of cunning and intrigue;
He buys a convert to set up for show,
As fowlers put a bird of painted wood
Within their nets, a lure to silly flocks
That flutter overhead, to draw them down.
Each day I feel his growing influence creep
About the king.   He and the queen have made
A royal convert; and he now hath won,
By promise of a kingdom and a bride,
This sordid, stupid Coifi to give up
His gods, and be a Christian, that the people,
By such example of their priesthood's chief,
May come beneath his cross.   I like it not;
For if Paulinus thrive, his rising star
Must surely dim my own.   I'll cross his path
With threads of cunning subtle as his own,
And pull his plots awry.   This plan of his
Would rob me of my princess.   Oh! what star,
Malignant to my fate, put this strange love
Into my breast?   I, who have made my trade
In probing human hearts, to feel my own
Rebel against calm wisdom with a longing
For this fair captive, that I cannot quell!
She is the bait that lures the priest of Odin

To sure destruction ; is she not a bait
To tempt me too into the same deep pit?
I see it yawn before me, but go on,
Drawn by her magic beauty—senseless fool,
To cry like a poor baby for the moon
Out of its reach !   I cannot have her love ;
She looks upon me with abhorrent eye,
And yet I sigh for her—nay, more : **will have her,**
If I lose all to do it.   'Tis a game
That I must play with every chance against me.

               Enter RHYN.

Rhyn, hast thou done my bidding?

RHYN.

                     Ay, my master.

PELLITUS.

Where is the captive princess? and what does she?

RHYN.

Waits on the queen.

PELLITUS.

           Her lodging, learned you it?

RHYN.

Ay.

PELLITUS.

With the queen's bower-women?

RHYN.

Ay, my master.

PELLITUS.

Watch her; watch all, even the silent mouse
That from a wainscot creeps for petty plunder;
Note how he thrives in his small enterprise.—
Do you know what I mean?

RHYN.

No little thing
Shall 'scape my eyes.

PELLITUS.

Ay;—go.

Exit RHYN.

He's serviceable,
And safe as serviceable because he knows
I hold his life in keeping.   Princess Enid !—
Have I indeed spent all my life for this:
To be as foolish as half-bearded youth?
My toiling feet have traversed distant lands;
My thoughts considered old philosophies
Of the dead Greek, of Egypt's older priesthood,

The lore of Brahmin and the imagery
Of Persia's wealth of fervent mysticism,
That, out of all, I might raise up a god
Unto my soul, the power of intellect ;
Now must I cast that symbol from its place
To set upon its pedestal a shape
So common as humanity—blue eyes,
Arched brows, bright golden hair of a fair woman,
Smooth cheeks of beauty rosy-tinted like
A lily blooming in the shade, but touched
By sunlight peeping through the leafy screen,
And painted with a delicate flush of red !
'Twas Helen's beauty broke the walls of Troy,
And Priam's daughter lost the son of Peleus !
Here in this island Cymrian Merlin fell
By woman's art—lured by her beauty, fell ;
An age of wisdom sunk in the short hour
He took the soft enchantress to his heart !
O, there was wiser thought in the Greek brain
That fastened round fair Venus' slender waist
Her cestus than my cold philosophy hath deemed !

   Enter GOLDDIN *and* BRIAN *disguised as a pilgrim.*

GOLDDIN.

Master Pellitus, your servant.   Shine the stars
Propitious ?—stars—ha–ha !—the stars.

To BRIAN.
>   Come, sir;
This is the king's magician; he will tell
Under what lucky planet you were born.
>   BRIAN *bows to* PELLITUS.

PELLITUS.

Who is this pilgrim? hath he not a tongue,
Good Golddin?
>   GOLDDIN.

>   Master Pellitus, no doubt
He hath a tongue; but it is vowed to silence—
Ha-ha!—to silence—ha!
>   *Exit* GOLDDIN.

>   PELLITUS, *aside.*

A pilgrim vowed to silence—under this
Is hidden mystery, and mystery   .
May hide a plot.   I'll watch, and set on Rhyn
To find out who this tongueless stranger is.
>   *Exit* PELLITUS.

>   BRIAN, *putting back his hood.*

It was the king's magician, him I seek,
Whose spells have been the brave Cadwallon's bane;
I must be watchful; one unguarded act
May bring upon me all this buzzing hive

· Of enemies.   How shall I find my sister?
I dare not speak, save to the pompous house-thegn,
Nor much to him.

> *Enter* RHYN; BRIAN *pulls forward his hood;*
> *aside.*

A Cymrian, on my life!—
A captured slave—I have a mind to trust him;
I will.

> *To* RHYN.

Thou art a Cymrian.

RHYN.

Ay.

BRIAN.

Of Gwynedd?

RHYN.

Ay.

> BRIAN, *throwing back his hood.*

Slave of the Saxon, art so much a slave
To yield thy prince into his enemy's hand?
Here in the stronghold of his foes he stands;
If, in thy heart, thou art indeed a slave,
Buy now thy betterment by his betrayal;
But if thou hast a spark of that bold spirit
That bade thine ancestors, with naked bosoms,

Raise up a bulwark on the ocean's edge
Against the Roman, give me helping words
To find my sister, and destroy the sorcerer
Whose spells have brought thy country many harms,
Baffling the wisest plans of Gwynedd's king—
Speak, Cymrian !

RHYN.

You are Brian.

BRIAN.

Brian, thy prince.

RHYN.

Your sister's with the queen.

BRIAN.

And Pellitus?

RHYN.

Beware my master ; he is full of cunning.

BRIAN.

Is Pellitus thy master ?

RHYN.

Ay, Prince Brian.

BRIAN, *raising his staff.*

This will I match against his wizard-wand.

RHYN.

Your stick's too little.

BRIAN.

Slave, it is the heart,
And not the weapon, makes a dangerous hand;
But art thou such a traitor that would stay
Help from his land, or peril from its foe?

RHYN *shakes his head.*

Thou fear'st his magic?

RHYN.

Ay; his cunning, more.

BRIAN.

How shall I see my sister?

RHYN, *after meditating.*

Tell the house-thegn
To bring you to the queen—if so you dare?

BRIAN.

Cymrian, thou hast some wit.   I come to dare;

So shall I see my sister—ha! away!
The sound of many steps—again, to-night.

> *Exit* RHYN; *enter the king's guard, then the*
> KING *accompanied by* EARL BLECCA, COIFI,
> PAULINUS, *and, after them,* GOLDDIN; BRIAN
> *muffles his head in his hood.*

KING.

We must consult with Pellitus to fix
A day auspicious.

PAULINUS.

Nay, your majesty,
Deal not with devils; if this Pellitus
Be not a crafty show of what he is not,
The slaves that serve him, and through him serve you,
Are wicked demons that will tempt you on
By giving what may seem like goodly service
Until you trust them much, and then betray.
What can be won from wickedness but ill?
Giving good service, is an act of goodness
The devil cannot do; who trusts to him
Takes Folly's hand, and shakes the head at Wisdom.

KING.

You give the dog an evil name, and then
Throw stones at him; although my dog may bark

Perhaps at Danger's shadow, yet his cry
Hath sometimes warned me well; I do not fear
His magic creatures.   Coifi, what say you?

COIFI.

Between the fall of Odin and the setting-up
Of these new gods my wits are so turned round
Old things put on new shapes; but Pellitus
Stands up outside of both these faiths,
And hath no part of either; so his wisdom,
Refusing both, hurts both, or hurts itself;
I do not well know which.   He hath been long
Your trusted counsellor, and given safe help
In many fortunes; how his knowledge comes,
From stars or devils, is too deep for me;
But help is help, nor would I fear his demons.

KING.

'Tis a bold counsel, be it wise, or no;
What says Earl Blecca?

BLECCA.

                    By Ella's magic sword!
Coifi speaks truth.   This wizard with his wand
Lifts up one corner of the mighty veil
That hangs between us and the coming days;

Peers with keen eyes into the deeps beyond,
And tells how sweeps along the endless train ;
What evils come, and how far off they be.
We listen to him, doubtful, or credulous ;
If his foretellings come, we are prepared ;
If not, we laugh ; but are not hurt at all.
It may be, as the learned bishop saith,
The work of demons ; but if serviceable
It is a sign that ev'n in evil things
May be a saving element of good—
Ay, there's no thing so utterly itself
It hath no touch or quality of another :
Night's pride of stars suggests the light of day ;
Day's secret caverns hold imprisoned night.

KING.

True ! Blecca, usefulness in everything,
Had we the wit to find it.   Honest Golddin,
Whom hast thou there so hid in pilgrim weeds ?

GOLDDIN.

Your majesty, 'tis one who, for a promise,
Hath sealed his lips up close—close lips—ha-ha !

KING.

Pilgrim, if thou hast not another promise,

To hide thy face, throw back thy masking hood,
And show thyself.

> BRIAN *bows low to the* KING, *but keeps his face
> covered.*

PAULINUS.

My son, if 'tis in penance
For some rash act, a guilt of burdened soul,
You go with covered face and silent tongue,
The king, at my request, will pardon you.

> BRIAN *bows again very low to the* KING *and
> bishop.*

KING.

Well, be it so; I like an open face—
A face like thine, my Golddin, free of guile.

BLECCA.

Your Golddin's face is like the sunflower's bloom,
That ever lifts unto the god of day
A bright, broad shape.

KING.

Or like the sun itself,
Shining at morning through a misty haze;—
We borrow poesy from thee, my earl.

BLECCA.

The eagle needs no song; his lordly pride

And majesty proclaim him, king of birds,
And make his piercing cry more fitting note
Than all the music of the woodland choir.

KING.

Do you not think, Lord Lincoln, that this bird,
The kingly eagle, may grow tired of state,
Weary of kingliness, and so pride-sated
That when he hears the evening coppice thrill
With the soft notes of singing nightingales
His monarch-breast will heave with fond regret
He was not born a songster of the grove
To pour his heart out in sweet melody ?

BLECCA.

I dare not say; the fashion of my heart
Is like the nightingale's, and not the eagle's.

KING.

Ah ! Blecca, much I doubt if majesty
Be to the eagle so much happiness
As eve's sweet carol to the nightingale—
My Coifi, beg this sweet-tongued nightingale
To sing for thee a song unto thy dove.

COIFI.

Not so, my king; the eagle's song for me;
If harsh his notes, he sings of victory.

KING, *pointing to* EARL BLECCA.

What think'st thou, Golddin, of my nightingale?

GOLDDIN.

My lord, I think his feathers are too fine,
And that he is not shy enough—ha-ha!—
Not shy enough.

> *Exeunt* KING, EARL BLECCA, COIFI, PAULINUS,
> *and king's attendants.* GOLDDIN *is stopped
> by* BRIAN, *who whispers with him.   Exit*
> GOLDDIN.

BRIAN.

Ay, I will kiss the queen's hand, paying homage
Unto the lady, not her sovereign power;
So shall I see my sister—my poor Enid!
How may her lone heart keep its native courage,
Here compassed round by enemies?   Brave sister!
What a big leap her little heart will make
If I can signal it!   The Christian priest
Gave me good help; I think this Cymrian face
Had startled them.   The slave of Pellitus—
'Twas rash to trust a slave; but not more rash
Than this rash undertaking; I have seen
The reckless win when the more careful failed.
Perhaps some spirit, unseen in the air,
Prompts the bold bosom to a perilous deed,

And helps its execution ; so I trust
My fortunes in thy hands, O guiding spirit,
That sittest throned above this desperate chance !
How shall I name thee ? Fortune ? Ah ! not so ;
I would not have thee wear the fraudful smile
Of her, the common mistress of mankind,
Who with caressing fingers blinds our eyes
While her dark paramour, Calamity,
Steals silently upon us.   Nay, fair spirit,
I will not slander so thy unknown name
To call thee Fortune.

Exit.

ACT II.

SCENE I.—THE QUEEN'S APARTMENT.

The QUEEN, ENID, *and ladies-in-waiting.*

QUEEN.

Who sang so sweetly 'neath our lattice window
At a late hour? I woke to hear a song
Mingle with plashings of the fountain till I dreamed
Myself in fairy-land. Methought that Merlin
Had built a magic palace, and I wandered
In its delicious gardens, while my eye
Saw brightly glimmering tower, and portico,
And lovely flowers, and clumps of clustered trees;
While over all the fairy moonlight streamed
With such soft radiance that its mellow flood
Made even enchantments glow more magical;
And all the while such dulcet sounds were ringing
In my rapt ears I scarcely saw the flowers,
The sculptured porticos, the moonlit trees,
The glistening towers; but felt them in my heart,
Blended with melody.

LADY.

The Lord of Lincoln
Sang to his harp last night beside the fountain;
Your majesty hath heard him.

QUEEN.

Was it mortal?
Sweeter delight to dream that Merlin's spells
Had fashioned for me an enchanted scene,
And filled it with the song of fairy-land;
But this were sin perhaps: my careful bishop
Bids me beware of fancies so profane,
Delusions framed by man's great enemy
To hide the truth; but in my infancy
I heard such tales from my old nurse's lips,
And they will haunt me ever with their glamour
Of bright romance.   Fair Enid, from thy land
Came these enchanted tales—but why so sad?

ENID.

The smile that curls a captive's trembling lip
Mocks at an aching heart.   Why should I smile?

QUEEN.

Princess of Gwynedd, is thy lot so hard,
To wait upon a queen?

ENID.

Nay, royal lady,
Not service, but captivity is hard.

QUEEN.

List; in his golden cage yon feathered songster
Warbles his melodies as joyously
As he could do in his far distant home
Beyond the sea.
                    ENID.

He hath forgotten home.

QUEEN.

Why cherish memories that bring but sorrow?

ENID.

The heart is memory.   A silly bird
May sing from empty heart gay joyousness,
Forgetting all except the golden sunshine
That glimmers down through flowers and   rustling
        leaves
To gild his cage with summer; but my heart
Can see no summer in the sun's bright rays,
No pleasure in these robes of regal pride,
No beauty in this golden cage, your palace.
My thoughts are far away on Gwynedd's hills

With my own people; or they fly still further,
And follow Gwynedd's king and my brave brother
Tracing sad steps upon a foreign land.
And you would have me smile? O royal lady,
My thanks are due for all these courtesies,
This rich attire more splendid than my wont,
A royal lodging, servants to wait on me,
And costly equipage. If I were free,
And in my Gwynedd, my vain, woman's heart
Would beat with joy to have such queenly state;
But here I am a captive, and this pomp
Seems to my heart an idle mockery;

QUEEN.

As much unto my royal lord, the king,
Thy thanks are due. Thou art a Cymrian princess;
And his intent—not yet perhaps matured—
Will send thee back to thy loved land, thy Gwynedd,
In greater state than when he brought thee thence.

ENID.

To Gwynedd? O dear lady! when?

QUEEN.

                              Nay, child,
I cannot tell; the king hath plans of state.

Enter GOLDDIN.

GOLDDIN.

Your majesty—the king !

QUEEN.

As ever welcome.

Exit GOLDDIN.

Ladies, we will receive the king.   Fair Enid,
Stay by my side.

Re-enter GOLDDIN, *ushering the* KING, EARL
BLECCA, COIFI, PAULINUS, *and the king's
attendants.   Exit* GOLDDIN.

QUEEN.

Good-morrow, my dear king.

KING.

Sweet queen, thy subject.

QUEEN.

Good-morrow, lords.

To PAULINUS.

My duty, holy father.

PAULINUS.

Bless thee, my child.

QUEEN.

> Earl Blecca, must we thank
> Your loyalty for an enchanted dream
> That your sweet music brought to us last night?
> Or were those magic spells of harp and song
> Designed for our fair princess?

BLECCA.

> Gracious lady,
> My harp and song are loyal to my queen,
> And to her court of beauty.   Nay, my spells
> May not be cast to work especial charm
> Upon your princess.   The Lord Coifi, lady,
> Sits up all night, and learns to thrum the harp,
> That he may be her minstrel.

QUEEN.

> What? Lord Coifi!

KING.

> Dear queen, we shall expect much gratitude
> For our good news.   This worthy Coifi, led
> By thy example and thy bishop's teaching,
> Hath come to know the true God from the false;
> He hath awaked out of a troubled dream
> To find those things are phantoms of his sleep

4

Which, while he dreamed, he fancied deities.
He will renounce the Norse gods, and with us
Call on the people to adopt thy faith.

QUEEN.

Most thankfully I bless the holy saints !

PAULINUS.

A light from heaven is shining on this land,
Whose pure, sweet rays, flooding the hearts of men,
Will wash away the stains of false belief,
And leave the truths, inherent in man's breast,
Faith, worship, veneration, homage, trust,
Cleared of the painting of idolatry,
To shine of their own crystal purity,
More beautiful than any artist tinting
Imagination's touch can put on them.
Here will we raise our church upon the site
Of Odin's broken altars, and the ruins
Of an old faith shall serve to build the new ;
For Truth sits ever on a past untruth,
More glorious that the thing she overturned
Was once deemed glorious. O great king and queen,
Your hands are blessed that ye can build this church,
Can send an influence of example out,
Will bring forth harvest, as the fruitful seeds,

Sown by a careful husbandman in lands
Broken and fallow by a winter's frosts,
Bring forth abundance in the sickle-time.

KING.

The land is ploughed; thou hast the fruitful seed,
And April rains are near.

To COIFI.

Put on thy apron,
My Coifi, for the planting.

COIFI.

Your majesty,
The people cannot choose but take this faith
When I shall say the Æsir gods are dead—
Dead of old age; that Midgard's mighty serpent
And fierce wolf, Fenrir, both in silence perished,
Subdued, destroyed, when on their fierceness fell
The shadow of the cross; that Surtur's torch
Went out, and left the world unburned;
While sun and moon, no more pursued by foes,
May calmly sail upon their radiant curves,
Or pause to shed more light upon the world
At His command, who hangs upon the cross.

BLECCA *to* ENID.

Your Coifi hath eclipsed the fame of Thor,
Destroying Fenrir and the Midgard serpent.

ENID *to* BLECCA.

My Coifi?

BLECCA *to* ENID.

     Ay.

KING.

     That all the world may know
How much we value Coifi's wise example,
We here proclaim that we will make him king
Of conquered Gwynedd, and will give its princess,
His royal bride ; so may he bring the land
To his new faith, and wear its majesty,
Subject alone unto our greater will.
Fair Enid, thus thy short captivity
Shall end in regal state.

ENID.

     My lord, the king,
I cannot wed Lord Coifi.

KING.

     Why?

ENID.
My hand
Is promised to King Penda.

KING.
Nay, fair princess;
The chance of fortune cast thee in our hands,
A captive; yet we make of thee a ward
Under our royal will.   The queen will tell thee,
Young maidens may not give their hands away
But by direction.   We would give thy land
Back to its ancient line, so the blue blood   .
Of its old royalty may fill the veins
Of future kings; but we must have a king
On Gwynedd's throne obedient to our will;
And we must have a Christian.   Of old time
Thy land was Christian, and again it must .
Bow down before the cross.   Be thou content,
Princess of Gwynedd, to accept the hand
Of him thy royal guardians shall direct;
Not pagan Penda, Mercia's warlike king,—
Reasons of state stand up 'twixt him and thee,—
But our King Coifi, to whose prudent care,
And thine, we give a kingdom.

ENID.
King of Deira,

I am a captive, not a subject ; pray you,
If you will seize upon my uncle's throne,
Give it among your people, not to one
Who would not keep her kinsman from his own.
Let the Lord Coifi place a Saxon wife
On Gwynedd's throne, not the unfortunate Enid,
Who will lament in a more lowly place
Misfortune's rigor to her land and kindred.

KING.

Princess, no more ; it must be as we will.

COIFI.

Fair princess, I would rather wed you than a Saxon.

ENID.

Thank you, my lord, for idle compliment ;
But my poor hand is pledged.

QUEEN, *who has overheard* COIFI.
                          What shall we think—
We Saxon ladies—of such choice, Lord Coifi?

COIFI.

My sovereign lady, think that Coifi blunders,
Being unused to ladies, love, and court.

BLECCA.

Think the Lord Coifi, most majestic queen,

Is like a child enchanted with a top,
And while he hangs above the whirling toy,
Forgets the world hath other toys than his.

QUEEN.

Ha ! my Lord Lincoln, art thou traitor too,
Calling thy queen a toy?

BLECCA.

                    Nay, nay, indeed ;—
Save as the sun, and moon, and shining stars
Are toys to children.

QUEEN.

                    Then is Coifi, child ?

BLECCA.

True ! madam, just born to your Christian faith.

KING.

Dear queen, this Blecca hath a subtle wit,
And claims beside to be a nightingale,
And calls our poesy an eagle's scream.

QUEEN *to* BLECCA.

Traitor again ; defend thyself, my lord.

BLECCA.

Lord Coifi's wit, great queen, defends me now.

QUEEN.

Lord Coifi's wit?

BLECCA.

He saith, the eagle's scream,
Though harsh of note, is tuned to victory;
Which makes the king a victor over song.

COIFI, *aside to* ENID.

Princess, think not I rather prize the throne
Than you.

ENID, *aside to* COIFI.

My lord, I am a slave, a captive,
Alone amid my enemies; be noble,
Generous as brave, and help them not to crush me.

Enter GOLDDIN *and* BRIAN.

GOLDDIN.

Your queenly majesty, a pilgrim begs
To kiss your hand, and kneel before your throne;
And—for he has a vow to hide his face,
And speak not—comes in silence—silence—ah !

PAULINUS.

It is in penance for a grievous sin
He hides his face, and comes with silent tongue;
It shows a contrite heart to put aside

The shows and pleasures of the giddy world,
And expiate a fault.

QUEEN.
Sir Penitent,
We thank you for your courtesy, and hope
Your pilgrimage draws near an end.

> BRIAN *kneels, kisses the queen's hand, and pre-
> sents to her a golden cross to which is attached
> a ring.*

A cross and ring !—my thanks.   Take this, Sir Pilgrim,
And count your prayers upon its golden links.

> *The* QUEEN *gives* BRIAN *a chain from her neck.
> Exit* BRIAN.

KING.
When next I wish to win a lady's gifts,
I'll go in silence with a covered face.

QUEEN.
Not so, my king ; with thee bare face will win.

BLECCA, *aside.*
So the queen pays a barefaced compliment.

QUEEN.
See this strange ring, dear king—a dragon's head
On a bird's body.

KING.

It is strange, fair queen ;
I know not what the quaint device may mean.
Earl Blecca, thou art learned in mystic things ;
Or thou, or Pellitus, must read this ring.

BLECCA, *after looking at the ring.*

Nay, king, 'tis not a nightingale or eagle ;
I cannot read it, yet the fashion seems
Somewhat to smack of Cymry ; it may be
The Princess Enid can decipher it.
            BLECCA *gives the ring to* ENID.

ENID.

It calls up to my mind pictures of old—
My father's palace, in one hall of which
Methinks a shape like this was cut in stone
Above the doorway.
        Gives back the ring to BLECCA.   *Aside.*
                'Tis my brother's ring.

BLECCA.

'Tis Cymrian, though perchance of so long past,
The thought once pictured in its curious shape
Is lost with the old thinkers who contrived it.
        Gives the ring to PAULINUS.

KING.

What says the wise Paulinus?

PAULINUS.

'Tis a thing
Born of a pagan thought; and doubtless comes
From far-off Egypt, land of worshipped birds
And monstrous beasts—ay, brought of old to Cymry
By some adventurous Druid who returned
From Eastern wandering to graft new gods
On the old stock of his idolatry;
But the graft failing, still the symbol lives
To mock idolatrous man above his doors
Or thus engraven on an ancient ring.
Gives the ring to COIFI.

KING.

I must entreat the queen to lend this ring
So mystically cut, and strangely brought
By unknown pilgrim, that my sorcerer
May mutter over it his magic spells
And bid his demons bring its history.

PAULINUS.

Still will you tamper with the spirit of evil?
O king, you seek the truth; no truth can come
Of evil; truth comes out of Goodness, God.

Of light comes light: the sun produces day,
And the night, darkness.   So will you be led
Into a fatal snare by Pellitus,
And see his devils mock and gibe at you.

KING.

There is no other way to read the ring;
Thy angels will not help me; I must try
His demons, or be left in ignorance,
As black a thing as are my wizard's imps.
If they would harm me, lo! I have thy cross
To scare them back into black halls of night.

COIFI, *who has been examining the ring.*

Perchance, O king, the bearer of the ring
May know its story; and there is a way
To change his silence into eloquence.

BLECCA, *aside.*

A barbarous—Christian that would murder romance!

QUEEN.

Ah, king, I pray thee do not hurt my pilgrim!
Thou wicked Coifi, half a pagan yet!

KING.

Fear not, my queen; he hath a shielding saint,

And none shall offer harm or insult to him,
Nor touch his mystery unless my Pellitus
Can pluck it forth out of this antique ring.

QUEEN.

Thanks, my dear king; all this is like a story
Which my old nurse would tell me long ago:
This pilgrim—mystery—and a strange ring;
I'll dream of it, and picture in my fancy
That Merlin weaves a spell about our court.

PAULINUS.

Rather, my daughter, learn to read the book
Sent by our holy father, and emblazoned
With pictured shapes of the immortal saints
And, on one cover in a silver glory
Set round with flaming crystal and with beryl,
The Holy One, the Lord and Prince of Love—
The Lord of Love kneeling to bless the world.
So let imagination dwell on Him,
And banish these vain thoughts of paganism.

KING.

Farewell, dear queen; we leave thee to thy musings
Of fairy-land and Merlin, or of saints.

Exeunt.

SCENE II.—AN ANTEROOM.OF THE QUEEN'S APARTMENTS.

Enter PELLITUS.

PELLITUS.

So ! so !—this ample curtain will conceal me ;
Beneath its folds I shall be safely hid.
Charms may do well to cheat the credulous,
But for the wise there's naught like native wit.
So I risk all; but desperate hurts are cured
By desperate remedies ; and this, my hurt,
Is past all cure save shrewd empiricism.
The garrulous house-thegn—whom I met but now,
And questioned of his errand—goes to bring
The pilgrim hither to a second audience ;
Here is a mystery that I must solve,
A secret motive I must puzzle out.
Who hath the secrets of a human heart
Hath half the power of the divinity
That governs fortune—ay, the better half.
I ask no magic of more potent force
Than knowledge ; having which, my human wit
Can stay, or faster turn, blind Fortune's wheel,
And act the fateful god—a key to power ;
And power I must have, or look idly on

While she, the thought of whom inflames my brain,
Scorches my liver like a fierce love-philter,
Will fly beyond the reach of wit or charm—
Ho! rustling robes—it is the princess comes;
So, while I wave my wand, I disappear.

> PELLITUS *conceals himself behind a curtain.*
> *Enter* ENID.

ENID.

My brother's ring and—as it flashed upon me
Like glimpse of torchlight through half-opened door
When I beheld that token—the same height
And bold, free step.   Brave brother, thou hast come
To set me free from this gay-painted prison,
Where danger masks in smiles and silken robes,
And bear me off to our free, native hills,
Where, through the heather, leaps the wild red deer,
And where the sky-lark sings a braver song
Than ever sung their love-sick nightingales.
Would he were come!   I must with watchful care
Keep down my heart, and school my prudent lips
To few, low words; one word too loudly spoken,
And overheard, might bring down unkind fate.
What a wise brother to so give his ring!—
Be still, my heart; he comes.

> *Enter* GOLDDIN *and* BRIAN.

GOLDDIN.

Fair princess, in obedience to the queen
I bring the pilgrim—what the ladies love,
A silent man !—a silent man—ha-ha !

ENID.

Thanks, my good Golddin ; thou art good as gold.

GOLDDIN.

To see your sweet face, is a purse of gold.
You are a stranger here, but all will serve you
For that same sweetness ; if you need a service
Golddin can do, count Golddin too your slave—
Your slave—ha-ha !

                     Exit GOLDDIN.

ENID, *running to* BRIAN.
O Brian !

BRIAN, *putting back his hood.*
           Enid, sister !
ENID *throws herself in his arms.*
Stay, stay thy tears, poor child—nay, nay, my sister ;
This heart, that flutters so upon my breast,
Seemed calm before the queen.   Be brave, my girl ;
We must be brave to win us back to Gwynedd.

ENID.

My brother, hast thou come to take me back?

BRIAN.

Ay, if thou wilt ; but thou art fine, my sister,
Robed like a queen ; perhaps this finery
Hath   won   thy   heart,   and   banished   thoughts   of
    Gwynedd?

ENID.

Brian, they deck me thus to make me queen—
The queen of Gwynedd.

BRIAN.

Thou, the queen of Gwynedd?

ENID.

Ay, Brian ; but they first would husband me
With the priest, Coifi, whom my heart abhors
With an unutterable loathing—ay,
Him would they set upon Cadwallon's throne,
And me, his queen.

BRIAN.

I understand it not—
Coifi, a priest, to rule our untamed people?
A priest of Odin may not carry arms.

5

ENID.

I had forgotten ; he is priest no more,
But hath become a Christian.

BRIAN.

　　　　　　　　Oh ! the bribe,
Thou and the throne of Gwynedd ; 'tis enough
To buy the fealty of a priest of Odin.
Now do I comprehend the speech I heard,
Of king and Coifi in the hall-of-waiting.
But we will mar their plans.　Listen, pale girl,
While I shall call the color to thy cheeks :
King Penda comes to claim thee of King Edwin,—
Ah ! now the lily borrows from the rose,—
But Edwin will not give his captive up ;
His Mercian vassal is too strong even now,
And such alliance might unvassal him.
So, sister, thou and I must fly to-night ;
I have my horses, stabled here hard by,
And friends at hand to help our enterprise.
At midnight meet me in the corridor
Outside these rooms, equipped for travelling,
And, ere the sun from saffron edge of hills
Springs to his daily journey, thou shalt be
Far from the perils of this gilded court.

ENID.

What joy to breathe the mountain airs once more,
And cast this shining queenery aside
For my own garb of Gwynedd's highland princess,—
But Penda—shall I see him?

BRIAN.

       Nay, my rose;
The Mercian king will ask thee of King Edwin,
Although he knows that asking is not having;
Or he hath reasons why he asks in state
For that he knows state-reasons will refuse him;
So state puts on formality ofttimes,
And pompous question, when the answer's known
Before the question's asked. I have not seen
King Penda; but upon my journey hither
One of his court I met, and learned, the king
Will come in largest state to offer ransom
And claim the hand of Gwynedd's captive princess.
What out of this may grow, I cannot tell,
But not thy freedom; so prepare to ride
With me to-night; meantime another purpose
Must have my thought: hast seen the king's magician?

ENID.

Yea, Pellitus; a man of wise, grave face,

Thought in his eyes, and cunning in his tongue;
He wears a wizard's gown, and bears a staff.

PELLITUS, *aside.*

She paints my picture; paint it handsomer,
Sweet princess—ha! what would the Cymrian?

BRIAN.

Enid, this man hath been thy country's bane.

ENID.

He ever looked most ugly to my eye,
Now will my thought give him a shape more ill
Than that he bears.

PELLITUS, *aside.*

O Cymrian, thou diest for this!

BRIAN.

Thrice hath Cadwallon sought to come again,
And, with good help of brave and trusty friends,
Set up his power in Gwynedd; but in each
This curst magician knew our secret plans;
King Edwin's men opposed us on the shore,
And forced us back to sea.   He hath a demon
Shaped like a sea-bird, black, with sail-like wings,

That flaps along the coast, and out to sea,
Who, when he marks Cadwallon's glinting sails,
Hastes with wild cries to Pellitus, his master—
Yea, it is true; I heard the fishermen
Tell of the uncouth bird, his gabbling screams,
And how the native sea-birds of the shore
Fly far, wild-shrieking, when his shadow casts
A spot of blackness on the bright, green waves.
Sister, for Gwynedd's sake the sorcerer's life
Must end to-night—nay, turn not pale, dear child;
This is my work; be thou in readiness
At midnight.

ENID.

Brian, Pellitus is wise—
Ay, wiser than thou deem'st; guard well thyself
If this thing must be done.

BRIAN.

Fear not, poor trembler;
But rest thee well; we shall ride hard to-night.
Now a farewell till midnight.

ENID.

Brother, farewell.
Exit BRIAN.
Brave Brian, how thy step belies thy garb!

Befriend him, powers unseen, that wait on men,
And shape the course of accident aright.
On what a little thread life hangs,
And yet so strong, a sea of circumstance
May dash upon it, and it will not break ;
Again, a careless word, a look, an act,
And, as a breath-puff tears a gossamer,
It is destroyed !—Alas ! my brother's life
Hangs by such perilous thread.

PELLITUS, *coming forward.*
                              You hold the thread
Of Brian's life.

ENID.
Oh !—Pellitus !

PELLITUS.
                    Ay, lady,
Your fair white fingers hold the shining thread
That reaches up from Brian to the stars.

ENID.
Mine ?—mine ?

PELLITUS.
Ay, yours and mine.

ENID.

How mine?

PELLITUS.

Thus, princess:
Content you Pellitus, and "powers unseen"
Will hear the prayer your sweet lips breathed to them,
And lead your brother safe from every peril;
Content him not, and they, the unseen powers,
Turning a deaf ear to your fondest prayers,
Will cast a snare for his unwary feet,
Falling by which, your brother's life is lost;
The fowler, Death, will twist his neck awry,
As the bird-catcher kills the fowls he nets.

ENID.

But how content?—

PELLITUS.

Fair princess, by your love.
Although my head be crownless, and this wand
No jewelled sceptre dazzling the eyes of men
With show of power, I ask and offer love.
Sceptre and crown are symbols; power is real;
Man is but man beneath his majesty,
And kingly state oft covers feebleness;

The while the energy that rules mankind
Hath oft no greater palace than a head .
Uncapped by golden circle ; nor a name
More splendid than my title, wizard—wise-man—
A title broader than the style of king.
Will you have gold? my gnomes shall bring you wealth
Enough to buy a kingdom.   Life, a queen's—
What is it?—vexation, sorrow, waiting, weeping,
A flitting joy or two, perhaps, to make
Pain's tooth bite deeper—pain, a reality,
And bliss, a myth.   Will you have this? or rather,
Instead of such a pain-enwoven fabric,
Sweet, magical enchantments, blissful joys
Beyond the fondest hope that ever thrilled
Young heart, beyond the most delicious dream
That ever made a passionate bosom heave
In the imaginative visions of sleep ?
Or, if you will, the majesty of power
Shall sit upon your brow : no queen in England
Shall have more noble state—a shining court
Whose gay magnificence the tongue of fame
Shall noise abroad.   Fair princess, give me love
For this good dower.

ENID.

Let me be dowerless,

And banish from your thought a foolish girl
Who hath no love to pay for such great gifts.

PELLITUS.

Princess, you mock me ; but my heart cries out
Against refusal.   Lo ! the stars proclaim it ;
And in enchanted runes 'tis written down ;
And spells and incantations promise it :
Fate interweaves our twisted threads of life.

Attempts to take her hand, which ENID *refuses.*
Nay, do not shrink.

ENID.

I cannot give you love.

PELLITUS.

I offer much in payment for your heart.

ENID.

Who would buy love, insults the heart's clear purity
With such base proffer.

PELLITUS.

What doth the lover offer
But barter of his heart of love for hers?
Lo ! this I offer you, and with a heart

As fond, as tender as e'er lover offered,
Magnificence, dominion, wisdom, wealth.

ENID.

I cannot buy this richness.

PELLITUS.

And your brother?

ENID.

I pray you, save him, and accept my friendship.

PELLITUS.

Nothing but love.

ENID.

I cannot give you love.

PELLITUS.

Listen : your face hath grown into my brain
Till all my heart hungers to have your love ;
It is a passion, a consuming fire—
Look that you mock me not ! I am not one
To sigh at woman's feet. Give my heart food,
And I will heap your lap with precious things
Till Fortune in amaze forget her blindness
To stare with envy from wide-opened eyes—
And, with such gifts, a love more rich than wealth ;

Repulse me, and you turn to direst ill
What, in your smile, were good.   Ah! can you love
The priest of Odin, in whose low-roofed skull
Thought lies asleep, while naught but animal instincts
Instruct the man? or Penda, Mercian wolf,
Who knows but war, and worships his own axe,
His highest notion of a deity?
In all that makes a man better than beasts
Am I much nobler than these twain.

ENID.

        O sir,
As you are nobler in a larger light
Of mind, be greater in your acts than those
Who know no purpose but to serve themselves:
Save my brave brother from his perilous chance,
Nor seek from me what is not mine to give;
In place of love take bounteous gratitude,
And let it satisfy your hungry heart.

PELLITUS.

I will not have it; 'tis to show the famished
A painted loaf, a carven form of food—
Ho, gratitude! a name, a gilded crown
The wise have made to top the head of Folly.
Lady, for the first time of all my life

I have laid bare my heart ; you have refused it ;
There is no more but this : what you deny
I yet will have.   Think not I speak in vain ;
'Tis not my habit, nor my use of words.
Look !   I will summon up all forms of power,
And work unseen, foreseeing what will be.
Farewell.   Your brother—you shall hear from him ;
But do not hope to ride with him to-night.

ENID.

Spend all your wrath on me ; but spare my brother.

PELLITUS.

Your love ?

ENID.

Ah, no !

PELLITUS.

All else is idle talk.

PELLITUS *is going.*

ENID.

Stay ! stay !

PELLITUS.

For love ?

ENID.

No ! no !

PELLITUS.

> Princess, farewell.
>
> *Exit* PELLITUS.

ENID.

My brother!—O my brother, I have slain thee!
What can I do? may I not seek the queen,
And tell her all? ah, still I slay my brother!
Unhappy Enid! how shall she escape
Or Coifi, or this dreadful Pellitus
Whose threats hang round her as the air were full
Of spying demons? Why delays King Penda?—
Reasons of state!—while these state-reasons stay,
Enid and Brian both may be destroyed.
Why swells my heart? what flashes on my brain?
Ay;—so at least I triumph over Pellitus,
And save my brother:—promise all he asks
When Brian shall be free, then with this dagger
Cancel rash promises. So shall I save
The richer of two lives;—but I will see
No more my Gwynedd; no more breathe the air
Blowing o'er heathery hills. So young to die!
And Penda—will he seek another bride?
Or feel regret state-reasons lost him Enid?

> *Exit.*

ACT III.

SCENE I.—THE KING'S APARTMENT.

KING.

The world outgrows beliefs: the boy becomes
Too big for last year's garments, slips them off,
And dons the new; in which he feels at ease
Until he gains the size that these allow,
Then they, too, pinch him.   Truth is back of all;
But truth, perhaps, would suit us quite as ill
As the man's raiment would a little child.
So we have grown beyond belief in Odin,
And legends suited to a former age,
Which cramp us now.   For sea-king and his band,
Sitting around the crowded galley's edge
Behind the wall of shields, to sing of Thor,
Or Freya's love-songs, while the salt waves flash
With dip of oars, or while the sea-winds sweep
Over the ridgy billows in wild gusts,
And screams the osprey circling round the mast,
Scared by a music wilder than his own,
Suited an age of heroes;—this is past.

'Though still by war I widen out my rule
Till all this island come beneath my sway,
Yet would I wean the hearts of men from war,
Building foundations of a steadfast peace;
And Odin's faith, that mocks at peaceful laws,
Must yield before the Christian.—Truth?—perhaps;
At least the change will give us present ease,
And that should satisfy our much-cramped souls.
With help of Coifi, who hath sold his gods
For a good price, I'll cast old idols down,
And build anew; so shall my people come
Into the garments of a larger faith.

Enter PELLITUS.

This Pellitus hath wisdom, not belief;
Or what he hath, he hides.

To PELLITUS.

Well, Pellitus?

PELLITUS.

Your majesty, I bring you back the antique ring.

KING.

O'er which your muttered spells have been in vain.

PELLITUS.

What would you learn, O king, of this old jewel?

KING.

First, I would learn from it of you; and then,
From you, of it.

PELLITUS.

My lord the king, this ring
Speaks with two voices: one, antique and weird,
Low whispering out of far-off halls of time;
And one, a present voice, here in your palace.

KING.

Each in due order.   What says its old tongue?

PELLITUS.

It is a legend of an olden king
Who prayed his gods to send him down a steed
From the bright team that draws the sun's hot car:
How the steed came, of monstrous size and shape,
Shining like burnished gold—a fatal gift;
For from his flashing scales such fierce rays flamed
They burned to cinder king and all his court;
Then the bright creature spread his golden wings,
And, meteor-like, flew back into the sun.
This ring was graven by an antique art
With shape like his in record of the marvel,
To show the figure of the wonderful steed,

And warn mankind to worship gods afar,
Not set them in their midst.

KING.

And old nurse-tale,
But in its heart a truth.—Ah! Pellitus,
May we not reach beyond the picturing
Of symbols to the truth?

PELLITUS.

The mind of man
Is fashioned so by Nature's cunning hand
It works with figures, and he builds him gods,
Wrought into shapes ideal, to satisfy
Desirings of his soul.   'Tis not the truth
Looks from his calm god's great, unwinking eyes,
Or mocks him in his symbols; but a creature
Of his own fancies born, their picturing.
The wisest thought, searching the farthest back,
Ends with a picture.   Life is a sliding row
Of pictures, bright and fair, perhaps, to one,
And rich with varied meanings that illume
Nature's broad purposes, and intimate
By subtle lips of beauty-breathing forms—
Process of mysteries—yet fairer visions
That lie beyond their shapes.   Unto another

Life is a senseless line of doubtful figures
That tell him nothing, promise nothing—blanks.
What there may be beyond these pictures, king,
I cannot tell.

KING.

So, then, your wisdom finds
No more than this?

PELLITUS.

The wisdom is to know
That these are pictures of the thoughts within us,
The lights imagination hangs above dark doorways,
But not outside of our humanity.

KING.

Well! of this ring: what is its second voice?

PELLITUS.

Its second voice is not an old nurse-tale;
It says: King Penda cometh to your court
To claim the Princess Enid; and it bids,
Pull off the pilgrim's muffling hood, and spy
The face of Brian.

KING.

Brian, the Cymrian?

PELLITUS.

Ay, king.

KING.

What brings him here?

PELLITUS.

He hath two errands:
The one, to snatch his sister from your court ;
And one, to slay your careful counsellor.

.

KING.

You, Pellitus? why you?

PELLITUS.

Because, my lord,
My watchful demon, flapping round the coast,
Hath spied Cadwallon's ships, and, warning me,
Marred every enterprise.

KING.

Good Pellitus,
Call up the captain of our guard.

Exit PELLITUS.

If this be true,
The wizard's demons are no idle help —
Demons ! nay, rather angels, thus contending

With evil; in themselves nor good nor bad,

But good or bad according to the wish

They help or mar, both good and bad at once

With two opposing wishes; 'tis to shift

Their quality from that wherein it should be

Into ourselves, if good and evil are

But in our estimation ;—humph! the thought

Loses itself in puzzling sophistry.

Re-enter PELLITUS *and captain.*

Captain, bring hither, under guard, the pilgrim.

Exit captain.

Ah! Pellitus, throw off th' enchanter's mask;

Tell me in honest truth how learned you this;

I doubt your demons.

PELLITUS.

Doubt! when the wind howls,

What stirs the elements to storm and rage?

What pushes over an invisible arch

The burning sun? why doth the pale moon shine

With altering phase? Do you doubt these, O king,

Because you cannot see th' invisible hands

That make each change? then wherefore will you
    doubt

Of my obedient demons? There are powers,

We cannot see, so subtle in their essence

That human sight grasps not their images ;
But what they do, as sunshine, lightning, storm,
Is so apparent unto conscious matter
That even the torpid earth feels their strong hands
Upon her, and cries, midst tumults, or midst silence,
"Lo! the gods move me, and send down their demons
To mark my bosom with a myriad fingers
That push up grass-blades, clothe the great-armed oaks,
Loosen white frost-caps on high mountain-tops,
Heave ocean into billows, sweep broad plains
With the great besom of the hurricane,
Or launch destruction with the thunderbolts."
O king, of a like subtlety, my demons
Mock at dull sight ; I show you their effects ;
If these be true, why not believe the rest ?

KING.

I cannot answer you.

Enter captain and BRIAN *surrounded by a
guard.*

Show me thy face.

BRIAN *stands motionless.*

Captain, unhood this ill-trained peregrine.

BRIAN *throws back his hood, and looks boldly at
the king.*

So we have found the face ; and now the voice ?

BRIAN.

The voice is Cymrian, like the face, and speaks,
What the face shows, a dauntless Cymrian heart,
Content to pay the forfeit of a life.

KING.

It is not much to take, but more to give.

BRIAN.

Not much to die.   The meanest soldier gives
His life in battle ; why should I, a prince,
Deem mine a greater thing?   The exile, king,
Sets no great store on life ; life is a thing
Of value, or of none, as it is stamped
By fortune or mischance ; he holds it best
Who loves it not too much, nor doth despise
The good it brings.

KING.

'Tis pity, Pellitus,
With him such wise philosophy must die !

PELLITUS.

One end meets all : Wisdom goes gravely to it,
While laughing Folly seeks it heedlessly ;
Pale Sorrow, in the midst of weeping, dies ;
Anger calms not the bluster of his rage,

Nor Jealousy forgets his haunting fiend,
In the last hour; and he, the calm philosopher,
Who speculates upon foreshadowed doom,
And sees its paths—his own among the rest—
All merging in one common ending, death,
Run o'er his careful plots and maps of life,
While pondering of it, meets the common fate,
And drops, or bears away, his cloak of thoughts.
I know not if 'tis pity; 'tis so common
That Pity, if she stand with streaming eyes
Weeping mankind, hath not one drop for each.
Though groans and wailing sound the symphony
Of death, this is but fashion of the world,
A loud lament for an imagined terror.

KING.

Cymrian, what folly brought thee to our court?

BRIAN.

The folly, king, to have a heart to love
My sister and my country.

KING.

        Rather the folly
To plunge in perils as the flitter-mouse
Flaps into brightness of alluring flames

That charm and dazzle his bewildered sight.
Ha! shall we hang thee up upon our walls
As, on his door, the ploughman nails a bat
Caught flitting impudently abroad by day?

BRIAN.

A noble trophy for a mighty king!

KING.

Captain, put this philosopher in chains,
And dungeon him, lest he commit more folly.
             Exit captain and guard with BRIAN.

PELLITUS.

O king, give me this young philosopher;
I ask him as a boon; not for his life,
For that I care not, nor am moved by touch
Of plaguing sympathy; but beg his fate
That out of him, as from his antique ring,
I may educe the plots, the unhatched schemes,
O'er which no doubt his friends now incubate;
So may I count the brood before they come
With ruffling feathers and their spurs full-grown
To crow, like chanticleers, before your gates.

KING.

I care not, so he trouble me no more.

PELLITUS.

My lord will trust me with his signet-ring?

KING, *giving his ring to* PELLITUS.

Ay, Pellitus; but bring not up this thing
To vex our queen.

PELLITUS.

His silence shall be real.

Enter GOLDDIN.

GOLDDIN.

Your majesty, the King of Mercia comes
With his attendant lords to greet his liege—
Now just arrived—arrived to greet his liege.

KING.

Ah, my good Pellitus, the ring tells truth !
Golddin, who waits?

GOLDDIN.

My lord, the Earl of Lincoln,
Lord Coifi, the queen's bishop, doubtless more.

KING.

Bid them attend ; call all our retinue ;
We will receive King Penda.

Exeunt PELLITUS *and* GOLDDIN.

Mercia's king

Will chafe to lose his bride—then let him chafe;

The needs of kingcraft smother sympathies

That else might blossom in a marriage feast.

Penda and Enid—were our promise clear

Of Coifi, none the less we must hold off

These twain, whose union might build up a power

Too great for vassalage.   The King of Mercia

Holds his head stiffly, bends not with a grace

Before our throne; this arrogance will grow

Greater, not less, unless we make him less.

So must we aim somewhat to prune his power,

Not to augment it with the strength of Gwynedd.

> *Enter the king's attendants,* EARL BLECCA, LORD
> COIFI, PAULINUS, *and lords; then* GOLDDIN,
> *ushering* KING PENDA *and his lords.*

PENDA.

Great king,

The tribute of my Mercia hath been paid

In deeds.

KING.

And worthily, O valiant Penda!

PENDA.

From its far southern line of sea-washed coast

I come to give you Wessex, subjugate,
And bowing humbly to your royal hand ;
A conquest well begun when on the head
Of wretched Cwichhelm, its assassin king,
Fell my keen axe.   The lesser limbs of war
Through his domain, back to the Cornwall hills,
Our Mercian arms have quelled.   Save Kent alone,
All Saxon England bends beneath your sway,
And Gwynedd's kingdom, with rich Anglesey,
And wild Welsh marches to the banks of Wye.
In these last conquests of the south, O king,
And all adown the line of Cymrian hills,
Mercia's bold hearts have done untiring service.

KING.

Most warlike Penda, well we know the worth
Of Mercia's help and thy heroic deeds ;
And, that we may show plainly to the world
How much we prize thee, we will bind thee to us
By the betrothal of our infant daughter,
The Princess Ethelfled, in the full hope
Thou wilt embrace the faith of all her kindred,
Leaving the broken idols of the Norseland
To bow with us beneath the Christian cross :
So shall this royal marriage one day bring
Unto thy sovereignty a third of England.

PENDA.

So great alliance, king, I may not have ;
My hand is promised, and my faith must be
That which my sires have held.

KING, *pointing to* PAULINUS.

      Nay, here is one
Will teach thee better faith.

PAULINUS.

      The God of Love
Is greater than your god of battles ; this, his cross,
A braver emblem than the hammer of Thor ;
The courage that can suffer, grander far
Than the rough daring of invulnerable gods.

PENDA.

Great king, I do not wish a better faith
Than my brave grandsire's, Crida's, who drew up
His stranded galleys on this island shore,
And from the din of Ocean's tumbling waves
Rushed amid Cymrian arrows to carve out
A throne in Cymry.   Ay, the gods, that gave
That throne to Crida, yet are strong enough
To help his grandson keep it.   Let me say,
King of Norse peoples, that my Mercians frown

And shake the head when flying rumor tells
Of a pale god set up above our Odin,
And his death-cross over our ancient altars;
That the priests find amid the smoking entrails
Strange prodigies, and mutter gloomily
With hoarse, thick voices, "Lo, there comes disaster!"
Unto your arm hath Odin lent his might;
The prize is won: will you forget your helper?

KING.

We may not brook thy barbarous people's threats;
The Æsir gods are tottering on their thrones,
And soon must fall.   To their old home in Norseland
Let them return, and build again Valhallas
Upon their Baltic shores.   Here will I raise
A palace unto Peace, and sheath the sword
To all but those who will not worship Peace;
And war shall end.   Our council sits to-morrow
Upon the question of a change of faith;
If thou wilt speak, King Penda, in the cause,
We promise thee a full and patient hearing.

PENDA.

I come not here to wrangle with your talkers;
You have enough to battle in such cause—
Those whose best use is in their use of words;

My strength lies in my axe, not in my tongue;
But I will hear your council, what they say.

BLECCA.

Doth great King Penda offer royal compliment
To the poor Lord of Lincoln?

PENDA.

Nay, gay lord;
We know your sword as keen as is your tongue,
Your voice in battle joyous as minstrelsy.

PAULINUS.

In the best fight man wages,—when his soul
Battles with Sin's fierce demons,—words have weight
Greater than your bright swords.   To hack and hew
The limbs of men, is not the largest purpose
That men can serve.

PENDA.

The goodly bishop calls me
From thoughts of war.   While in the south I fought
To make its conquest good, your arms in Gwynedd
Achieved success; in conquered Worcester
The Princess Enid fell into your hands.
King, I would ransom her; she is betrothed

To me; my kingly promise pledged to her
Hath made me seem to slight your royal favor
And great alliance.   If my wars have been
Worth any recompense, I ask but this:
The right by ransom to redeem my princess.

KING.

King Penda, Gwynedd's princess fell to us,
The spoil of war; we knew not thy betrothal;
But have bestowed her on our servant, Coifi,
Whom we will place with her on Gwynedd's throne.
Our royal word is pledged.   If the Lord Coifi
Will take thy ransom, thou mayst ransom her;
But we may not.

PENDA.

What should a priest of Odin
With princess? or with throne?

KING.

A priest no more:
He hath abandoned his idolatry;
Hath cast off priesthood for a laity;
And we, his king, give him a throne and princess.

PENDA.

'Tis little honor now to be a king,
If priests wear crowns.

COIFI.

And wherefore not a priest ?
Your famed descent from Odin loseth rank
As Odin, his ; thus you go down, priests up.

PENDA.

A brainless fool !

KING.

Ha ! will ye quarrel, lords,
Before our throne ?

PENDA.

I quarrel not, O king,
With this vain fool that wags his tongue at me—
King Crida's grandson bearded by a priest !—
King, I have done you service, and for payment
You give me scorns; are these the meed of service ?
To-morrow will I speak of this again,
If I can rule my tongue to measured tones,
For now my heart's too hot to coin cold words,
And time must cool it.

KING.

Penda, though thy speech
Lack something of respect, we pardon it
For that hot temper urges reckless words,
And that we value worthily thy service.
To-morrow shall thy question have due audience.

Meantime, accept our hospitality :
Our queen would thank thee for heroic deeds
That fame hath heralded out of the south,
Noising thy glory ; wilt thou come to her?
Ourself will bring thee.

Exeunt.

SCENE II.—A CHAMBER IN THE QUEEN'S APARTMENTS.

ENID.

"Pain, a reality ; and bliss, a myth."
Are his words true?—Too true ! too true with me !
How this dull gloom settles about my heart !
I'll sing away its dull despondency
As the poor cageling sings :

Singing.

An ethereal spirit of the mountains
Loved passionately a maid,
But pitiful sorrowing laid
Full many a lingering trace
And cloud on his beautiful face,
For his shape was invisible to the maiden.

7

Though he hovered caressingly o'er her,
    And whispered of love with fond word,
    Her ear all-unheedingly heard
    No voice as with gay heart she sang
    Till evening's soft zephyr-airs rang
With her carols of youthful rejoicing.

Then he cried to the woodland and mountains,
    " Alas and alas, she heeds not !
    How strangely unhappy my lot,
    So near her, and yet far apart
    In distance of heart from her heart,
And my tenderness never made known to her !"

" Mother Nature, why was I made loving,
    And not of a visible form ?—
    To feel all love's passionate storm,
    And die for a beauty I see,
    Yet, living or dying, to be
But a viewless and voiceless desiring !"

Ah, why do I remember such a song
Of loneliness, when I should sing gay notes
To drive away the sadness of my heart ?

            Enter a lady.

             LADY.

The queen will not require your presence

At evening audience ; but she bids me say,
She will desire you sing to her at later hour.

ENID.

I note a bustle in the anterooms ;
Is there a ceremony?

LADY.

Ay, an audience :
The queen receives King Penda and his lords,
Our king and lords likewise.

ENID.

I thank the queen.

Exit lady.

They bar me from his sight while ceremony
Hath due observance.   So the world goes on :
Formalities must pass, though hearts are torn
And lives are spent.   Here is sharp agony,
And by its side the courtly bow and smile
And empty nothings, idle ceremony,—
To kiss the queen's hand while they make of mine
A thing to purchase converts to their faith !
Why should King Penda dally with court follies?
While he procrastinates, quick fate comes on,
And gives me up to Pellitus, the priest,
Or death.   Why asks he not to see his bride?

Is he, too, purchased by this gilded court
That smiles, and buys?   It were an act of manhood
To tell them to their courtly, smiling faces,
He will have nothing at their hands but me;
They would not dare deny him;—but perhaps
Gay smiles of court beguile his thoughts of Enid,
A captive; and her country conquered, spoiled,
He seeks a richer bride;—alas! no hope!
Why should I strive with fate? ah! why not yield
To either chance, and smile as the world smiles,
And see in life but hollow ceremony?—
N o my free, Cymrian blood disdains to flow
Along the sluggish lines of their court-usage:
I'll save my brother; then come Death between
The purchase and the payment—
                         Enter RHYN.

                              A Cymrian face!—
Who art thou that, with unknown features,
Bring'st back remembrance of my far-off home?

                         RHYN.

I'm Rhyn, the slave of Pellitus.

                         ENID.

                              Alas,
A Cymrian and a slave!   My native hills,

Do you breed slaves to serve your Saxon lords?—
What wouldst thou, slave?

RHYN.

My master, Pellitus,
Bids you come to him when the night's dark hours
Hush all in sleep; or, ere the light of morn,
Your brother, Brian, dies.

ENID.

Where is my brother?

RHYN.

Deep in a dungeon, shackled fast with chains;
And Pellitus, my master, wears his master's ring,
And holds your brother's fate.

ENID.

O! tell me, slave:
Is there no way to save my brother's life?

RHYN.

Ay, if you please my master.

ENID.

Say:—I will;
And come for me at midnight.

RHYN.

Lady, ay.

RHYN *withdraws, stepping behind a curtain.*

ENID.

A few hours more of rosy light will shine
On wretched Enid ; then must come the night
Whose darkness will o'erwhelm her.   While they laugh
In the queen's presence, king, and lords, and—Penda ;
Or the Lord Lincoln sings, and sweeps the harp-strings,
And Ceremony sits the queen of all ;
Here do I watch the fast-declining day,
Waiting for Night to wrap me in her folds,
And bear me off, sad, lost, companionless,
To ghastly halls of death ; where, clothed anew
In different form,—perchance uncouth or hideous,
Some creature that I now would shudder at,—
My spirit will inhabit a new form,
And live unconscious of this thing I am,
And Enid be forgot.   Will he laugh then,
When they shall hurry o'er my funeral rites ?
Or will he drop one tear upon my grave ?
Or will he think of the more happy bride
They promise him ? alas ! I may not know.—
What if my hand should falter at the last ?

Takes a dagger from the folds of her dress.

No; rather a thousand times this shining blade
Than Pellitus!—

RHYN *advances.*

RHYN.

Ho, princess! will you slay

My master?

ENID.

Slave, begone! it is not midnight.

RHYN.

No; I must speak :—a woman, dare you die?

ENID.

Ay, slave; but, being a slave, thou knowest not
What such words mean.—Heed not this idle trifling;
'Tis fancy's fitful light that dances here.

Points to her head.

RHYN.

Fancy?—crazed head?—The flashing of her eye
Is not the fire of weak or crazy wits.
Lady, I was a servant of your house,—
Ay, long ago, when you were but a child,—
And did a thing, for which they drove me forth,
And I became a slave. Though years have passed,

I feel the old love tugging at my heart ;
And if a thing so helpless as a slave
Can help you now, it may atone the fault
That banished me of old.   I know not well
What I can do, but I will study it ;
And chance may help a slave to serve a princess.

ENID.

Forgive my unkind harshness, generous slave.

RHYN.

Fair princess, may I kiss your royal hand ?
'Twill help me to a thought.

> RHYN *kisses* ENID'S *hand, then exit.*

ENID.

Why doth a hope light up my desolate heart
With the slave's words?   It is, his sympathy
Leaves me not all alone.   What was the tale
My old nurse told ?—how once a little mouse
Gnawed at the strings that held a netted lion,
And set him free.   Perhaps this is my mouse.   *Exit.*

ACT IV.

SCENE I.—THE KITCHEN. EVENING.

DAGBERT *and* RHYN *sitting at a table on which stands
a great beer-jug.*

DAGBERT.

We must consider it well, Rhyn; for the conscience
be a tender thing, and easily scratched. I say often to
myself, " Dagbert, take care of thy conscience; thou
be'st but a jailer, it is true; yet a jailer's conscience
be a thing to be cared for." If it hurts him, he turns
as uneasily in his straw, look you! as the king in his
golden bed; for this same conscience careth not what
bed he sleeps in.

RHYN.

You speak shrewdly, Master Dagbert; and, because
you are known to have a wise head——

DAGBERT.

Ay, ay, Rhyn; I be one that thinketn of many
things. [*Takes up the jug and looks into it.*] This

talking be dry work, and the jug empty.   I fear Master
Cook will not fill it again.

RHYN.

I have here a broken penny which my master gave me
long ago ; I cannot use it better than for my conscience.

DAGBERT.

No, by Neccus ! that be well said, Rhyn—[*Taking
the money.*]   Ay, a half-penny.

RHYN.

I dare not go to Master Cook, for I broke a jug
sevennight ago, and he still looks black at me ; but ·
he will look white at you, Master Dagbert, when he
sees the silver.

DAGBERT.

The jug shall be filled, and thy conscience set right,
if there be any wit here.   [*Pointing to his head.* DAG-
BERT *takes the jug, and goes out.*]

RHYN.

Another jug of beer will drown what wit
Yet flickers, like a storm-wet, smoking torch,
In his dazed head, and cast him in such stupor
He will not wake though Faul, his Saxon demon,

Shout in his ear; then will I have his keys,
And be Prince Brian's jailer.   Let me think—
She said : I, being a slave, know not what thing
It is, to dare to die ;—well ! do I dare?
I know not; but I feel a something here
That drives me on; it may be it will push
So far as dying.   Dare I plot to thwart
My demon master ? boldly match my little
Against his much ?   To wind about his plans,
And cross their cunning, I should be more cunning
Than he whose quick eye, flashing in my face,
Will catch the coward thought I try to hide,
And flout it to my ear.   In spite of him,
His magic, demons, spells, and sorcery,
I'll set my stupid brains against them all;
And if I fail—ah ! it perhaps may be
I dare to die, and know not that I dare.
Here comes the jailer, drunker than before.

Enter DAGBERT, *with the jug of beer, and singing.*

DAGBERT.

The king may sit in golden state
    A golden crown to wear,
But what care I ?   I am his mate!—
I have no crown for my rough pate;
    But this shall lift me there,

Beside the king—above the king—
This pot of beer that now I sing.

Rhyn, thou serving-man of Ochus Bochus, don't think
because I sing, I be drunk—no ; I sing for jollity—
ha-ha ! [*Puts the jug on the table, and sits.*]   Now
listen : if what old Ochus Bochus doeth be sinful,
and he be in danger of roasting for it, as our lady's
bishop sayeth, then thou, being his helper, shall be in
danger of roasting too ; this be reason—plain reason,
look you, But to go deeper into it : [*Takes a long
drink from the jug.*] Ochus Bochus, being a wizard,
may by dry-craft get himself out of the fire ; but will
he pull out his helper ?—will he pull out his helper ?
[*Drinks.*]   That be the thing to be thought of.   See
here : Ochus Bochus [*Drinks*]—Ochus Bochus—it be
all here [*Pointing to his head*], but twists round and
round so, by old Neccus ! I ben't able to pull it out
straight.

RHYN.

'Tis dry work, pulling against a wizard.
—Master Dagbert, drink up the beer.

[DAGBERT *drinks, then staggers to his feet.*]

DAGBERT

I have it now ; listen !—Ochus Bochus—Ochus—
ha-ha ! ha-ha !

[*He sings.*]

Old Neccus, from thy cave
And thirsty salt-sea wave,
Come up! come up! come up!
Old merman, here's to thee!
Come, tip the jug with me;—
Come up!—come—up!—come—up!.

[DAGBERT *staggers against the table: tries to
drink; oversets the jug, and tumbles on the
floor.* RHYN *stoops over him, and searches in
his leathern sack for his keys, but fails to find
them.*]

RHYN.

I cannot find the keys; his sack is empty—
Misfortune! so to lose it, when I thought
This chance was safely won!—what now?—how?—
    how?
Have they, my master's cunning demons, come,
Sliding unseen their thin shapes under shadows,
And stolen away the thing I would have stolen,
Snatched up the prize, and borne it to their master?
No! no! it cannot be. Ho! drunkard, wake!
        Shaking DAGBERT.
Wake! wake!
      DAGBERT *raises himself on his elbow.*
      Your keys, good Master Dagbert,—keys!

DAGBERT.

Old Ochus—Bo-chus—come—up!—

RHYN.

Where are your keys?—your keys!
    [DAGBERT *falls back, insensible.* RHYN *shakes
      him again and again, without result.*]
He will not rouse.   I thought to steal his keys,
Lead Enid to the dungeon, free her brother,
And, stealing from the palace, fly with them
Beyond this nest of dangers; but my plan—
A good one if I had this drunkard's keys—
Is spoiled or e'er begun.   What is there else?
O that my head had but a little wit
To make new plots!—one chance, and that one lost
Without my master's stir!   I know no other.
Now do I think I am not all a slave;
For, while I find no way to win by craft,
My heart grows big; I feel my bosom heave,
Thinking what I must do: I am resolved
To strike a blow for her, though it must be
To rush, like famished wolf with open mouth,
On death.   But wait; some chance may help me yet;
If not, what better end for Rhyn, the slave,
Than dying at a beautiful princess' feet?   *Exit.*

SCENE II.—THE DUNGEON. MIDNIGHT.

BRIAN *chained.*

BRIAN.

It cannot be his gods that heap his fortunes
High as the hill-tops,—yea, they grow so huge
This island gives its greatness but to him,
All other kings belittled,—for his gods,
And those of all his ancestry he scorns,
Seeking to cast them from their ancient thrones,
On which to set a cross.   'Tis Pellitus,
By stars and magic, lifts the King of Deira
Thus over all.   Alas, my dear-loved land !
I ventured all to cross a demon's path,
Against his spells opposed a zealous heart,
And so have lost.   Nor for myself I groan ;
But much for thee, and something for my sister,
Who, proud but gentle, hating slavery
As water, fire, must be the gilded slave
Of this king's policy—no, not a slave ;
Not all of England's power can break her spirit
Into a slave's obedience ; it will flash
Out of her free heart as the dark cloud gleams

With sudden fire, and scorch the ceremony
Would chain her to a bondage worse than this.
                    Raises his chains.
Lost Enid! their vile schemes will ring thee round
Until escape is shut, and death alone
Can give a refuge.   A soft woman's heart,
That quails at desperate act, is not the lodging
For a free soul in these dark days of peril;
It should be set in some strong citadel,
Apart from danger, if the arm to strike,
The eye to look on perils, undismayed,
Are given her not.   A man may laugh and die;
But death hath greater terrors to a woman,
Frighting her timid breast.   Oh, fie upon it!
Where is the gracious power that governs life,
And loosens out the tangled skein of chance?
Is ill, not good, the thought that works the scheme?
Can it be so: that man is ruled by demons
With naught to check them? then, indeed, his life
Is a poor thing, too worthless for regrets;
And all the greater hopes, that heave his bosom,
Are misplaced here; and I may hail the hour
Of death that sends me down the chain of being,
Haply to wear the various garbs of life,
And glide from shape to shape, nor ever find
One of less worth than this!   If life in each

Be overruled by evil, let me haste
To reach the end, if end there be—a scheme
Unworthy all the intricate adjustments
With which it moves before our dazzled eyes—
A tedious ladder, up or down whose steps
Demons may chase my spirit.   Let me sleep,
And dream perhaps of greater things than life.
Pshaw ! thoughts of Enid make this dungeon-floor
A restless couch.   Nay, but indeed I'll sleep.

> *Enter* RHYN, *carrying a torch, then* ENID. RHYN
> *fixes the torch in a sconce on the wall, and
> exit.*

ENID.

Dear Brian, I could weep upon thy chains
Till the hard iron, melting with soft pity,
Dissolved in my hot tears.

BRIAN.

       Ah, tearful Enid !
The moisture of a dungeon eats these chains
But tardily ; thy tears of tender loving,
Though full of alchemy for human hearts,
Will fall effectless on my stubborn gyves.

ENID.

If they have alchemy for jailers' hearts,

8

Their floods shall pour like our own mountain streams
Fed by great storms.

BRIAN.

Nay, tears avail not, Enid.
I hoped to take thee out of Danger's clutch,
And risked a life of little worth to me,—
Thou in captivity, and Gwynedd conquered,—
In the rash chance with glad enthusiasm.
Now, when that chance hath failed, my chiefest sorrow
Is that I cannot save thee from the toil
In which, poor bird, thy fluttering wings are caught.

ENID.

It matters less, my brother, what disaster
May hap to me, a useless, fluttering bird,
Fit only for a song of joy or sorrow,
Than thus to bring in peril thy brave life,
Rich in the hope of help to our dear country.

BRIAN.

I thought to help our Gwynedd, and help thee,
My sister; but all fall alike the prey
Of Pellitus. O that this arm of mine
Were long enough to strike him from these chains!
So would I deem I won in the exchange,
My life for his.

ENID.

Thy life hath larger worth.
Brian, I come to give it thee again ;
For thou art dead in chains, and freedom, life.
Although my tears may not dissolve these irons,
Yet can I free thee ; not indeed with weeping
Or sorrow, but with smiles.   Thy life is dear
To Gwynedd ; and I, ev'n I, a snared and trembling
    bird,
As thou hast said, dear Brian, have the power
To give my Gwynedd a great boon, thy life—
Prince Brian's life—his who will gather up
The fortunes of his land, drive forth the spoiler,
And wear, perchance, our ancient Cymrian crown.
Then Enid, though forgot by all but thee,
My brother, may, in thy dear remembrance held,
Share in thy glory ; for she breaks for thee
These dungeon chains that else, beneath their weight,
Had crushed down hope and life.

BRIAN.

Thou ravest, sister ;
Sorrow hath crazed thee, falling on thy spirit
As some strange phantom comes amid our dreams
To push aside all customary thought
With the improbable.

ENID.

Nay:—Pellitus
Is of my suitors; and, at my command,
Must touch these cruel chains with magic wand;
His alchemy, more potent than my tears,
Will set thee free.   Ah! smooth thy brow, whose
     frowning
Contends with wonder working on thy face—
Thou shalt not owe him aught; 'tis I that free thee.

BRIAN.

I am amazed, and marvel not that wonder
Traces its outward figures, for within
It fills my mind with frightful, grotesque shapes;
This Pellitus stood by with sneering lip
When the king questioned me, and, by the looks
Which flashed between, discovered to my thought,
Who had denounced me.

ENID.

Ay, 'twas doubtless he;
He lurked, a spy, behind the drooping curtain;
Watched us, concealed; heard every word we spake,
And learned the purpose of thy hapless visit.
Not love of thee, but hope of better favor
With me, whose better favor he would have,

Shall work the help I bid ; but count no chance
Upon his mercy ; he is merciless,
Strong in his cunning, wise as pitiless.

BRIAN.

Sister, beware ! seek not to match this fiend
In cunning ; as the serpent charms the bird
Till, with enchantment drugged, it, powerless, falls
In the wide jaws that gape for it ; so he
Will charm thee helpless.

ENID, *aside.*

        Oh, protect me, Macha,
Mother of gods, from this most loathsome charmer !
To BRIAN.
Nay, trust me, Brian, woman's wit will match
His wisest cunning, though with magic helped,
And spells of sorcery, the shine of stars,
And all the glamour of a conjurer.

BRIAN.

Nay, Enid, think not thus to play the masker,
Hiding thy thought beneath unmeaning words.

ENID.

Incredulous ! You will believe my power
When I strike off this weight of heavy chains.

BRIAN.

Enid, thy quivering lips mock such wild speech;
Beneath the flicker of this smoky torchlight
I see the painful lines of high resolve
Stamped in thy face; pray tell me what they mean.

ENID, *aside.*

I dare not tell him; and I wear my mask
So illy that he sees my pallid face beneath.
To BRIAN.

What can I tell thee? 'tis a woman's plot:
This wise magician—but not wise in this—
Is smitten with my face; a woman's plot—
He seeks my favor, and I use his help,
Buying with idle promise thy dear life.

BRIAN.

What dost thou promise him?

ENID.

                    A little thing,
A woman's favor.
BRIAN.

                    It is a thing too great—
By far too great; for its entanglement
Will close about thee as the fowler's net

Catches the bird that hath a pair of wings
To fly above the snare, but cannot use them.

ENID.

Brother, farewell; I must not stay to hear,
And be affrighted from wise purposes.
When I shall send the keys to loose thy chains,
Fly from the precincts of this hateful palace,
And use the life, that I have given to thee,
For our dear land.   I see a certain way
To slip between the meshes of the net ;
But think of me sometimes.   Now kiss me, brother.

BRIAN, *embracing* ENID.

So now I have thee, sister, in my arms,
Thou shalt not go till thou hast told me all :
What is this mystery? what, the wise plans
With which thou think'st to baffle Pellitus,
A giant in the cunning use of craft ?

ENID.

Nay, kiss me, brother ;—if I hoped to win
By the straight line of an unchanging plan,
Thy wisdom should o'erlook the careful scheme ;
But when a woman plots, her figures shift
Faster than fashion of dissolving clouds,

And every moment brings new policies.
So is she strong, because no reach of brain
Can tell her changes.   Thou art helpless, chained ;
I dare not trust thy wit ; kiss me, dear brother,
And let me go.

BRIAN.

Thy heart beats hard, my sister,
Like the poor fawn's who sees the bounding dogs,
And hears the cry of all the noisy pack
Draw near—

ENID.

O Brian !

ENID *bursts into tears, and sobs convulsively.*

BRIAN.

Weep, poor child ; if tears
Can bring thee comfort, on their swelling flood
Let sorrow float out of thy sad, bruised heart—
Yea, weep thy fill ; and when hot tears are done,
Tell me the thing thou vainly seek'st to hide.

ENID.

O brother, how unloving ! know'st thou not,
To lose thee from my sight, to be alone
With strangers, meet strange looks, and hear strange
      voices,

Are cause for sadness? and that woman's tears
Gush easily from loving eyes at partings?

BRIAN.

Ah, Enid! I had not believed this thing
Without such plain and manifest disclosings
As speak to me from ill-dissembling features
And voice unschooled to feign the thing that is not:
That thou couldst so have paltered with my love,
Hiding thy purpose under subtle seemings.
Did I not know thy crystal purity
Beyond the thought of question, I might deem
Th' intent dishonest, over which thou hold'st,
With so unskilful hand, a doubtful mask.

Enter RHYN.

RHYN.

My master!

Exit RHYN.

BRIAN.

Enid, alas! I fear thou art
Upon the brink of a great precipice
So high, I dare not look to its perilous foot;
The while, perforce, I wear these pitiless chains,
And hug this wall. I see impending fate

Above thy head, but cannot reach my hand
To stay it.   As the spirit of man, set free
By death, may hover over those dear ones
He fondly loves, but cannot help, so I
Look on the face of dire calamity
Approaching thee, without the power to shield ;
And see : it comes—

Enter PELLITUS.

PELLITUS.
                    Fair princess, give me pardon
If I must rudely cut the tender endings
Of fond farewells.   I would not bid you part
Too hastily ; but in the night's deep sleep,
As in the noisy day, swift hours move on ;
And soon loud-crowing cocks and baying dogs
Will waken early stirrers.   If to-night
We break these chains, and set a captive free,
He soon must be astir, ere curious Day
Pulls off the cloak of much-concealing Night,
Beyond the outlook of this busy York.

ENID.
It needs but one last word, and we will part.

BRIAN.
Why must we part ?   If you will render service,

Do it not piecemeal.   Pellitus, I thought
No power could stay the hatred of my heart
And peril of my hand from you ; but, lo !
I offer to quench both, so you will give
My sister freedom ; nay, I proffer friendship
And honored place,—whatever you may choose,
Less than the crown,—to buy your magic help
For my dear Gwynedd.

PELLITUS.

                    Still you squander time,
Seeking to purchase what is like the time,
Not upon sale : so shut the chapman's pack.

BRIAN.

Thus may you be to Gwynedd's valiant king
What Merlin was to Arthur, and your name,
A glory and renown above all names !
Honored with a brave people's love and reverence,
Your life be filled with fame ; and after death
The years bear on your glory, fadeless still,
And by undying legend made immortal.

PELLITUS.

You offer payment with a generous hand,
Dipping it deeply into future years,

And scattering images of glittering shine
Before my eyes.   These are not yours, rash youth,
To offer.   What ! do you think to startle me
By novelty?   Know, I have pondered well
Fame's promises, and, weighing carefully
The future, found it hath not anything—
Nay ! in its sum of all, not so much value
To buy this flitting instant of the present.
I do not choose to bargain for a name.

BRIAN.

What can I offer for my sister's ransom?

PELLITUS.

Nothing to me ; your own is all the question
That brings us here.

ENID.

         And I—can I say aught,
Proffer you aught, the price of present freedom?

PELLITUS.

Not now ; I give you here your brother's life ;
Nor dare I venture more, for weighty reasons
Importing much to me.   I, whom he sought
To slay, give him his life and liberty.

ENID.

How shall I know my brother hath good speed
After our parting?

PELLITUS.

Do you doubt me, lady?
Here are his keys; myself would loose the chains,
But, knowing well your brother's rash intents,
Fear present freedom may induce to folly
His headstrong youth.   While I attend you, princess,
My slave shall be his servant to unlock
These fetters, and conduct him where a steed,
Saddled and bitted, waits a rider's spur
To give him safety, as quick-growing miles
Leave death and danger conquered by his feet.
Is this well, princess?

BRIAN.

Nay; it is not well—
I answer, Sir Magician, for the lady.
I will not blindly serve dark purposes,
Although they lead to present liberty.
I came, as you have overheard, to take
Your life for harmful spells your magic wrought
Against my Gwynedd; I have failed; my life
Is fallen in your power; take it, magician.
I will have naught of you—naught but the thing

I came for; failing that, will not receive
Thus doubtfully from hands of an enemy
My life.   The stake is lost; take it, magician.

PELLITUS.

As winning gamester, throwing for a chance
Of larger ventures, lets his smaller stake
Remain unclaimed, so value I the fortune
That makes me winner of your life, a thing
As valueless, 'twould seem, to you, as me.   .

ENID.

Brother, from me—take life a gift from me !

BRIAN.

So it would come from him by second hand.
I marvel, sister, that you give him heed,
And sully honest thought with so ill converse.
I should despise myself, a tainted thing,
Soiled by his giving, if I could content me.
To owe him life.

PELLITUS.

                 The chances of the world
Make life depend so often on those things
We would not choose to rest our lives upon
If we had choice, or power to govern chance,

That, if we so could gather soil from others,
All were, as Ethiops, black ; and nature, foul.
Is the white lily's purity defiled,
Or the rose-blossom's perfume made less fragrant,
Because decay lies fetid at their roots?
This is vain Folly's lightest, idlest humor,
Which giddy youth mistakes for nobleness.
I know not why I cross your mad caprice
To say that folly's folly—'tis alike
To me if folly bid you live, or die.

ENID.

I ask thee, brother : Brian, live for me ;
Nor, for a fancied harm, abandon life
To meet harm's dread reality—so, flying
Disaster's painted counterfeit, thou fallest,
Scared by a threat, into the yawning gulf
Of true calamity.   We may repent
Of a wrong choosing, and repair the fault,
If we have life ; but he, who chooseth death,
Cuts off repentance and a second choice.
Thou smilest, as to say, " The death I choose
Is easy for me" ; if it be indeed,
Then art thou choosing what is easiest,
Leaving to me the hard and painful task
Of battling with the world.   If I could look,

As thou canst, with untroubled eye on death,
Untrembling see the doomful gate swing back,
Closing behind me with its dread " Forever,"
Then would we die together ; but I cannot.
Take not away my only hope of help,
Throwing thy life disdainfully away—
Why ! this is cowardice ; it is true courage
That bids a great heart bravely dare to live.

BRIAN.

Ah ! sister, wouldst thou see a Cymrian prince
Loosed from his chain to fly like frightened hound
With racket at his heels?   Brave help to thee
A fugitive could give.   No ; I will die
Here like chained bear pining for native wilds,
Or baited to his death by snarling dogs.
Sister, no more ; thou shalt not buy my life.

ENID, *throwing her arms round* BRIAN.

Brother, my tongue hath tempted thee with lies:
I dare to die ; I will not part from thee ;
I thought to buy a richer life with mine,
And willingly—yea, willingly !   O Brian,
Keep me beside thee ; I will gladly die !

PELLITUS.

Excuse me, lady, but this may not be ;

I brought you here to save a brother's life,
And not to die. If he will not have life,
The fault lies not with me, but with himself.
I cannot give a longer waiting: princess,
Speak your farewells, and speedily, I pray.

ENID.

I will not go with you.

PELLITUS.

     Are you both mad,
That thus you heap one folly on another,
Mock me with idle caprice, changing moods
Absurd as fancies of a petted infant?—
By Juno! lady, do not tempt me further,
Lest I forget respect for Cymrian princess
In the behavior of a heedless girl—
You will not stir? Princess, I bid you come.

BRIAN *to* ENID.

Enid, what wilt thou do?

ENID.

    I will not go.

PELLITUS.

By wing-foot Mercury, a pair of fools,

That cannot see they have no power to say
"I will" or "I will not"!   In place of Parcæ,
I hold your threads, to twist them, or to break,
As I may choose.

BRIAN.

A frowning, angry Fate—
Enid, they will not load thy arms with chains,
But there are shackles, as I fear, whose chafe
Will cut as deep.   I cannot help thee—go;
And good, kind spirits guard thee; go.

ENID.

No! no!

PELLITUS.

Ho! Rhyn!

Enter RHYN.

Bring me the lady hither, Rhyn—
Stay not a moment; bring her here, I say.

RHYN *endeavors to bring away* ENID, *who clings
to* BRIAN.   PELLITUS *drags her away by force.*
So wilt thou tempt me, princess? yea, thy touch
Sends the quick blood like fire along my veins!

ENID.

Loosen your hands; I'll go back to the queen.

PELLITUS.

Bend not upon me such an angry eye;
Is this the promised favor? By the zone
Of Venus, I will have a kiss!

ENID.

Help! help!
ENID *draws a dagger, but, before she can use it,*
PELLITUS *takes it from her, and throws it*
aside; RHYN *picks it up.*

BRIAN.

O mighty Ogma, burst these cruel chains!

PELLITUS.

Ho! lady, wilt thou scratch? I swear by Venus,
It were a fault to leave thy lips unkissed!—
A fault to Venus and her cooing doves—
A fault to beauty and its dimpled loves—

ENID.

Help! Brian, help!
RHYN *stabs* PELLITUS *with* ENID'S *dagger; the*
magician releases ENID, *and, drawing a sword,*
turns towards RHYN, *but falls.*

PELLITUS.

The slave—oh, folly! folly!—
To hold the chances fairly in my hand,
And lose them thus!

RHYN.

Where are his demons now?

PELLITUS.

The slave, a Cymrian!—stupid, fatal folly
To overlook this chance! but chance is fate,
And fate is sure to meet us face to face
At last—is this the last? how dark it grows!
Why have you quenched the torch?—blood—so much
    blood!
Can this be death? and life so quickly creep
Out at a little gap?   The dungeon sinks—
O Death, thy mystery!—mystery!—no more—

      PELLITUS *dies;* RHYN *takes his keys, and unlocks*
      BRIAN'S *chains.*

BRIAN.

Brave Rhyn, a royal blow!
        The chains drop from him.
            Faint, faint, my sister?
Nay! let me chafe thy hands.

Enter KING PENDA *muffled in a cloak;* BRIAN
seizes the sword of PELLITUS.

Who art thou? speak!

PENDA, *throwing back his cloak.*
A friend, Prince Brian.

BRIAN.

Penda, King of Mercia!

PENDA.

The Princess Enid!—this is strange indeed;—
And a dead body, dabbled in its blood!
Takes the hands of ENID.
Dear princess, thou art deathly pale, and shake
As if with ague.

ENID.

'Tis with fear, my lord,
And foolish fancies.

BRIAN.

Marvel not; this riddle
Is quickly shown; but first, what brings you here?

PENDA.

King Edwin's guest, I learned of your mischance,

And, under cover of this cloak and night,
Came secretly.

ENID.

   Pray take me hence ! I tremble,
And shudder yet with fear ; while Fancy whispers :
" The dead magician may return to life,
With bloody hand beckon a frightful demon
Out of the shadows that the torchlight flings
Against these walls"—see ! see ! he moves !—
Take me away, I pray !

PENDA.

Pale trembler, come.

BRIAN.

He only moves, my sister, in thy fears ;
This Pellitus is harmless now ; his demons
Forsook him at the last—Ay, we will go ;
And I will tell thee, more at leisure, Penda,
The night's strange chances.

To RHYN.

     Come, my friend ; to thee
We owe much more than thanks.   *Exeunt.*

ACT V.

SCENE I.—THE GREAT HALL OF THE PALACE.

The KING *and* QUEEN *in chairs of state; beside the* KING, EARL BLECCA, COIFI, *lords, and* GOLDDIN; *beside the queen, the Princess* ENID, *ladies,* PAULINUS, *and priests. In front* KING PENDA, BRIAN *disguised as a Mercian noble, Mercian lords, priests of Odin, etc. At sides and back, guards and attendants. On one side an armed figure representing Odin; on the other, a great crucifix held by a priest.*

KING.

King Penda, we have shown thee more at length
Our purpose in this council; and once more
We ask thy voice and that of Mercia's lords
Upon the question; freely give full speech;
Let every Mercian help us with wise words
Fairly to weigh our purposed policy.

PENDA.

O king, we better know the ways of war

Than peace, the use of arms than sounding words ;
Myself and fellow-soldiers are more skilled
To swing the axe than wield an argument ;
For we have oftener heard swift arrows sing,
And javelins clash upon our ringing shields,
Than these word-battles : nathless will we hear
The wise opinions of your counsellors,
And give our own rude thoughts in ruder words ;
But, ere these larger purposes appear,
I ask again, great king, in modest guise,
My suit, the ransom of the Cymrian princess.

KING.

We would desire, and grant thee, larger asking
With a glad heart, free hand ; nor scant thy worth
In word or deed.   Unasked, we proffered thee
Greater alliance than a Cymrian princess ;
But so you name a thing beyond our reach
Unless we will revoke our kingly word,
And take again what we have freely given,
Which must not be ; for kingly majesty
Shows kingliest when honor lights its acts,
And justice shines, the jewel of its crown.

PENDA.

I turn from such stern judgment to the queen,

And place my cause before her gentler court;
If rough the advocate, not so the suit:
Must passionate pleading yield to cold decrees?
Fair queen, reverse the judgment of the king.

KING.

We are content the queen shall give an answer;
Our sentence is not wrought of arrogant will,
But through its woven web shine golden threads
Of bright amenities.

PENDA.

Must Mercia supplicate in vain, fair queen,
Your tenderness? Raise up a humble suitor,
And make his hopes as bright as your fair face.

QUEEN.

We thank King Penda for his offered tribute,
But florid compliment wins not his cause;
For in my heart, as in the wise opinion
Of my lord's court, religion sits enthroned
In highest seat. Love lasteth for a day,
The soul forever. Kneel before the cross,
And you shall win yourself an advocate
More loudly voiced than are a hundred loves;
But ask me not to give our captive princess
Into a pagan's keeping.

PENDA.

Queen of Deira,
I cannot sell the ancient faith of kings
To buy my princess.   Once you gave the keeping
Of a sweet princess to a pagan's hands ;
And, lo ! the gift will prove a means to bring
The pagan to the cross.

QUEEN.

So might it prove
With you if wedded to a Christian wife ;
But not when both are pagan.   Giving Enid
A Christian husband, gives therewith the hope
Of one day coming to her husband's faith.

PENDA.

And my appeal hath failed ?

KING.

Take wiser thought,
And ask a larger thing.

PENDA.

What thing is nearest
The heart seems greatest, as an outstretched hand
May hide a mountain : I will have no other ;
Refuse me this, and you refuse me all.

MERCIAN LORD.

Great king, our Mercia puts her claim for service,
Done in your wars, into King Penda's hands;
Denying him, your nay will coldly strike
The hearts that warmly beat with loyal zeal.

KING.

Our nay is given. A royal pledge must stand
Against all murmurs. Let Mercia ask a thing
Honor may nobly give, and our great giving
Will show how rich we prize its loyal hearts.

Rising.

My lords, the present purpose of this council
Hath been set forth, and many well-weighed reasons
Beforetime given. For these recited reasons,—
Wherein the virtuous precepts of our queen,
And fair example, with the patient teaching
Of her most reverend bishop, have great place,—
And for a certain sign, directly shown
In a strange vision, from my heart I cast
The old religion of the Æsir gods.
But while I feel great hands of Supreme Power
Pushing Bor's children from their old-time thrones
Within my heart, yet do I challenge Awe
And this new Potency with anxious question.
We hold in royal hands a people's weal;

And may not change, as doth a fickle mind
With a new thought, unless such change will bring
Our people good.   So have I studied well—
As careful pilot looks on shore and sea,
On flying clouds that tell how move the winds,
On the strained mast that bends with each wild blast—
The fortunes of my land.   The lips of Odin
Breathe war in every legend of the past,
And tell the future glory of Valhalla
Filled with resounding arms.   Must war prevail
Perpetual? and these valleys and green hills
Be but the camps of armies?   No; my thought
Looks forward with the forecast of the seer,
And welcomes Peace, a goddess of bright hopes,
In place of blood-stained Freya—valleys, hills,
Melodious with the lowing of fat kine,
Fair towns, rich cities, built by port and stream,
And, yellow in gay meadows, waving corn.
This cannot Odin bring; the clash of arms
Makes barren fields, and towns and hamlets burn
Upon the track of War.   You know me well :
I am no coward, trembling at the flash
Of gleaming steel, that thus I find a thing
Better than war.   From the rough northern hills
Beyond the Tweed, where roam wild, native tribes,
Down to the Cornwall coast, my sword hath won

A sovereignty ; I now would sheathe its edge,
And cherish, not destroy.   When long ago,
A homeless boy, I dwelt at Cadvan's court,
And later, when the murderous Ethelfrith
Hunted me forth as dogs drive out a wolf
From shelter of his den, my mind would dream
Of a glad time, far off in future years,
When, lord of this wide land, I might lay down
My victor sword, and bid sweet Peace arise
To spread enchantments as the sun pours light
Brightly upon broad realms.   That hour is come ;
Cast down the warring Odin, and seek Peace
With me beneath the shadow of the cross.

QUEEN.

Sweeter than sunshine doth that shadow fall,
And the glad earth, marked by the holy sign,
Smiles with delight ; the little grass-blades smile,
And lovely flowerets wear more delicate tints,
Kissed by the shadow of the crucifix.
                    To PAULINUS.
Stand forth, my holy father, and declare
Unto these lords the mission of our Christ.

PAULINUS.

O king and lords, the throne of the Most High

Is set above the great blue vault that domes
The wide-spread earth; where with a shining host
Of angels, seraphs, cherubim, dwells He,
The Lord of all, Creator of the world.
Man is His creature, with a bodily form
Shaped by His hand, a consciousness of soul
Fashioned in faint resemblance of His own—
Man is His creature, by His boundless love
Encircled as a green and lovely island
Is held in fond embrace of the caressing sea.
But man knew not this love; his feeble sight
Turned upward, lost in azure depths of space,
Reached not the throne of Heaven; but in the gleam
Of sunshine, light of stars, the glimmering sheen
Of ocean, breath of meadows rich with perfume,
Murmur of insects, smiles of hill-sides
Glad with harvest, merry songs of birds,
Tumult of tempests, impress of haunting dreams,
Chances of war, disease, shipwreck, and death,
He felt the power that mocked his reach of sight.
Then artist Fancy fashioned curious myths,
The progeny of legendary wonders
Descended from the past; and in their hands
Placed the great sceptre of the God of Heaven.
But He, above, looked down with pitying eye
On man's rude fancies and absurd beliefs;

As He had given His creature being, now
He gave a richer gift, the light of Truth.
Descending from His throne, in human shape
He came to be man's teacher, and His theme—
Whispered beforetime by the voice of nature,
But to deaf ears—was His unbounded love.
To seal that love, and bridge the abysm of space
Between His throne and earth with human sympathy,
He took upon Him man's infirmities,
And gave His body in sharp agony
To perish on the cross.   Behold the sign !
                    Points to the crucifix.
.What better token of a love divine ?
What purer teaching than a scheme of love ?
See ! from His cross, this God looks down on you ;
O turn from worship of your cruel Odin
To the sweet face of Christ, the crucified !

            QUEEN, *pointing to Odin's statue.* .
See how dark Odin frowns with angry brow,
                Turns to the crucifix.
While love beams forth from Christ's angelic face !

                PENDA.

If pitiful Love ruled in the hearts of men,
Your god should sit o'er all ; but tell me, queen,

When we have cast aside our warlike arms
Who shall protect us from the northern tribes,
Or from our viking cousins, o'er the seas,
Who know not this high sovereignty of Love,
But put great faith in Odin, god of battles?

PAULINUS.

When foes assail, upon the breast of Peace
Hanging War's panoply, ye may go forth
And conquer in the name of blessed Peace.

PENDA.

If it be name alone, and you can change
Your white Christ to a warrior, let us try
To teach our Odin how to be a saint,
And keep our ancient faith.

KING.

                    No saint of Odin
Can come of teaching.   Odin is only war,
A breathing of the spirit of savagery
Born of the stormy North.· Gay Lord of Lincoln,
Tell us: the life of man, must Odin rule it?
Or may we govern our brief staying-here
And going-hence by this new creed of love?

BLECCA.

O king, this life of man is a strange marvel.
Amid the whirl of days that bear us on
Through ruined years, events leap up, and cry,
"Lo, this is life!" but while we listen each
Wild cry grows faint, and dies.   We seek to look
Beyond the present, peer with curious eyes   `
Among vast shadows; but, beholding naught,
Ponder on pictures of an endless time
Stretching—we know not where.   From such huge
    shapes
Turning bewildered, we come back again
To our to-day, nor less bewildered, ask,
"What is this life?"—O king, it is a scene
In your great hall at the mid-winter feast—
From a heaped pile of burning logs the flame
Roars in the chimney; cheered by genial warmth
Sit king and queen, your thegns and ealdormen;
Here there is light and heat, but out-of-doors
The fierce storm raves, and whirled by howling winds
The snow drives wildly to the snow-piled earth.
Lo! through the door—opened by careless groom
To note if winds abate—flies in a bird,
A waif of nature, homeless in the storm.
With frightened wing it circles round the hall,
But quick is gone again into the night

10

Through the rent casement's gap—gone into night,
And seen no more.   This sparrow is man's life.
While it is here it feels not freezing winds
Dash storm and darkness on its weary breast;
The blazing fire is flashing in its eyes,
And warmth and comfort rather mock its flight
Than mark its stay, while fear and destiny
Hurry it forth into the stormy night
Where it is lost.   We saw it here, a thing
Little to us; but, to its own scared heart,
A mystery of greatness.   Whence it came,
Or whither gone, we scarcely may conjecture;
Out of the black, tempestuous night it came,
And back returned; a moment fluttering here,
And then no more.   Though doubtless ere it came
It had a history, and afterward
A fate accomplished in the howling night,
Yet what they were, we know not.   This is life;
And we, such night-lost birds.

QUEEN.

Poor bird! poor life!—so it is pitiful.

BLECCA.

Tell me, O priests, if you have heard it whispered
By rigid lips of great ones in some hour

When they have broken through accustomed silence
To prattle with you as companions talk,
Or as the wise give lessons to green youth ;
Or if 'tis written in your sacred runes ;
Or lives, the moral of some ancient legend ;
Or muttered down from priestly lip to lip:
Where hath my soul been wandering ere this life?
Or whither flies it when death's winter night
Shall hide it from your eyes?—Odin tells not ;
Nor, as I fear, your Christ can answer this,
Save in vague pictures, unrealities,
That dimly show an unsubstantial seeming.
If all beyond this life be but a blank,
If forward, backward, both ways end in night,
To me be given the laugher's merry creed,
And let me flutter my gay wings in light,
And shun the tempest, and avoid the night.
If I must choose or War, or gentle Peace,
A frown, or smile, I rather choose the smile ;
Count me a convert to the god of Peace.

QUEEN.

Ah ! Lord of Lincoln, in my dreams to-night
I shall behold gigantic shadows chase
Thy night-lost bird, fluttering on failing wings,
Into a black and shunless destiny.

PAULINUS, *pointing to the crucifix.*

Here is a refuge in the heart of Love
From storm, and night, and death.

KING.

Wise Lord of Lincoln,

Beneath thy painted mask of poetry
And skilful picturing of words appears
Question too great for our philosophy:
The ceaseless wash of nature's waves, the years,
Laves with uprising crests our solvent lives,
With sinking ebb bears off a part of us
Into the sea of time.   Afar that sea
Looks smooth as summer lake, more near in storm
It breaks on man, a billowy dash of spray
And so wild tumult of mad agonies,
That death is rest and haven from its rage;
But storm or rest, a constant menstruum
Of human life—that life, for briefness, like
The fleeting moments a spent swimmer keeps
His head above the vast and pitiless flood:
Then shall we see, in death, a hand of Love
Stretched upward mid the boiling waves to save?
Or some huge kraken that all-hungrily
Sucks us adown to its insatiate maw?

PENDA.

A nobler picture, if so brief be life,
A javelin's flight : it sings along the air
From Odin's hand, and, crashing through shield-rim,
Dies there, blood-drunken; to be caught anon
Out of pierced shield, and wing again its flight.
But, to my mind, this life hath space enough
For largest honors: if my hap to fill it
With glory such as Crida greatly won,
Then glory shall assume enduring shape
Like lordly palace builded to the skies,
Speaking from lips of sculptured blazonings
Valor's great acts; its shining pinnacles
Neighboring the stars; its fame enduring ever
While love of glory stirs in hearts of men.
Nay, it is idle prattle of life's shortness;
Life is too long if filled with idleness;
Quite long enough for Valor's high renown
And thoughts and acts that live renewed in breath
Of minstrelsy, immortal in a song.
Lo ! in the hall, the hungry feast is over,
And kitchen-knaves bear off the empty platters,
While warriors loosen belts, and cry aloud,
To fill the horn, and send it gaily round.
Then while bright drops are sparkling in each beard
The king calls up his minstrel, bidding him

Pour forth the soul of glory on the flood of song.
Now while he sweeps his harp, all bend intent
To catch sweet notes ; but when in swelling tones
He sings of glory, lo ! the warriors rise,
Push back huge benches ; from bright baldrics pull
Their great swords out, and while the torchlight flickers
On flashing blades, shout till the oaken roof
Sends back, each rib reverberate with din,
A great response to glory.   Life is short?
Nay, it is great and deathless when it lives
On minstrel lips, thus summoned back again
From hollow vase, sea-cave, rich, marble tomb,
Or the rough cairn that marks a hero's grave—
Ay, deathless through all fortunes save the chance
Of glory's death in man's degenerate heart.
What is the tame existence of dull years
Though stretched by magic through unending time,
Crawling from bed to food, from food to bed,
Compared to life eternal in the breath
Of song?

QUEEN.

So would you drown each gentler note,
That Peace may sing of sweet affection's joys,
In drums of battle. Pray, most warlike king,
Why do you seek a queen? a carven thing
Cut of white ivory, and crowned with gold,

Would fill your chair of state.   O, set not there
A woman of warm heart, to feel that heart
Crushed in such iron keeping, if you know
No dearer yearning than a victor's hope,
No fonder thrill than comes of glory's song !

PENDA.

My picture hangs with others on the wall ;
What time hath frightened bird, or a spent swimmer,
To dream of love ?   Turn your reproachful eyes,
Fair queen, on him of Lincoln and the king ;
Perhaps my heart hath pulse of love as great
As either.   These are only pictures, lady,
And mine no more reality than theirs.

COIFI.

I see not why we trifle thus with pictures
When great realities come face to face
With idle fancies, pushing these shadows forth
Out of our hearts.   Too long have worshipped pictures
Held our obedience.   Look, how Odin stands,
Picture of might !   If he were might indeed,—
Not hollow seeming, empty, shining armor
Set up in fashion of an armored man,—
Would he not leap from marble pedestal
To smite our sacrilege ?   I long have served

This idle god; have set before his face
The fairest things ; upon his altars burned
Gifts of great price ; the blood of slaughtered captives
Poured at his feet ; but yet he stood as now,
Only a picture ; and the power, I dreamed
Shut up in his mailed bosom, never once
Gave me a sign ; yet still I served, and worshipped,
Until the light of this new faith shone down,
And day dawned in my soul.   Then I beheld,
In place of deity, an empty figure,
A shell of form and nothingness within,—
Nor like a shrivelled acorn with a germ
Of future life,—while prayerful at its feet
Knelt many nations offering sacrifice,
Burning rich gifts, and shedding human blood.
This sight, so strange, awakened my contempt ;
I laughed at it, and, filled with scornful ire,
Snatched the great lance-shaft from his nerveless hand,
And beat his helmet till the roof-tree rung
With noisy clatter, and the dinted brass
Bent with my blows.   O lords, is this a thing
To worship, this dull god that may be beaten
Like any drunken slave ?

PENDA.

Blaspheming dog !

Doth the round moon heed every snarling cur
That yelps at his great disk?

A Priest of Odin.

Hear me, O king!
Nor deem great Odin's sleep, the sleep of death:
Worn with long vigils, at his mighty foot
I slumbered; waked to hear an awful voice,
Deep as the thunder,—while blue lightning played
About his helmet,—bid me bring his shield,
The sculptured stone a hundred men in vain
Might strive to move; I marvelled, but obeyed;
And when I touched the ponderous block, it stirred
As light as gossamer, that there I hung it
On the left arm of Odin; then he cried,
"Sleep on," and at his word I fell asleep;
But when I waked, looked upward tremblingly
Where on the arm of Odin still there hung
The carven stone—Then I cried out; at which
It fell with frightful sound as if the wind
Split into tatters an enormous sail;
And I beheld the marvellous shield roll back
To where I took it up; and many heard
The great stone fall, came hastily, and saw
The form of Odin shake, blue tongues of fire

Still flaming round his helmet, while I lay
In terror at his feet.

COIFI.

A stupid dream !—
This god is moveless, voiceless, powerless.
Behold, I wage my arm against his might !
Give me an axe, and I will smite this image ;
If it be not the senseless thing I say,
Let it smite back ; but if I cast it down,
And stand unharmed, I have dethroned the god.

KING.

Give him an axe.

> *One of the soldiers of the king's guard gives an
> axe to* COIFI, *who advances to the statue of
> Odin.*

COIFI.

So fall the Æsir gods !

> COIFI *raises the axe to strike.*

PENDA.

So Odin strikes !

> PENDA, *with a sword-thrust, kills* COIFI, *who
> falls at the feet of the statue of Odin.*

KING.

O traitor !—Ho ! my guard !

The lords of Deira draw their swords, and,
with the king's guard, press forward; the
Mercian lords close about their king with
drawn swords; while KING EDWIN *advances*
in front of PENDA. BRIAN *leads* ENID *among*
the Mercians.

PENDA.

Here. at your feet, O Christian king, I cast
My vassalage. Set up your cross of Peace
In Deira; Mercia knows no gods save those
Our fathers worshipped—"Traitor," do you say?
Nay, I am true unto my ancient faith,
And will not serve a traitor. There lies one
　　　　(*Pointing to the body of* COIFI.)
Whose purchased hand presumed to soil his god
With its vile touch—one, you would make a king
For treachery; he was unkingly ever,
And past your kingly power to crown him now.

KING.

Thy head shall lie as low!

PENDA.

　　　　　　Then shall these halls
Be red with slaughter. I have filled your court
With Mercians, and will cut a bloody track

Back to my land.   I ask nor peace, nor war;
But stand prepared alike for either chance.

KING.

A monstrous rebel!

QUEEN.

Dear my lord, I pray thee,

Turn not thy court to a wild battle-field;
Because I am no warrior, swords affright me;
Let the fierce Penda and his Mercians go.

KING.

Let it be so.

To KING PENDA.

We give thee safely forth

To Mercia; there full well defend thyself;
For, by yon crucifix, we swear to plant
The cross in every village of thy land!

PENDA.

Red will the soil of Mercia grow, O king,
About your plants.   I take this offered truce;
And for the Princess Enid, who will go
With me to Mercia, will return the price
Of a king's ransom.

KING.

Nay, we give her thee,

All ransomless, in payment of past service;
We would not owe an enemy so much
As is thy due; and thus we cancel it.
So, having paid old scores, we now may feel
The only debt we owe is present due
Of bold rebellion.   Go; the path is clear
That leads to Mercia.

PENDA.

Mercia, by my hand,
Now breaks her chains; no recreant to the gods
Shall claim her service.   For this courtesy,
Your gift of Gwynedd's princess, 'tis set down
As a new debt to courtesy; all debts else
Cancelled, my country oweth naught but this.
Now, King of Deira, Penda, King of Mercia,
No more a vassal, giveth his farewells.
He gaily bids you to his wedding feast,
You and your court—a welcome unto all;
Or choosing rather war, come with your hosts,
. And still he promises a kingly welcome.

Exeunt.

THE END.